A HORSESHOE CRAB COVE CHRISTMAS

M. LEE PRESCOTT

A Horseshoe Crab Cove Christmas

By

M. Lee Prescott

Published by Mt. Hope Press
Copyright 2021, M. Lee Prescott
ISBN: 978-1-7379034-4-4

Cover design by Ashley Lopez
Image credits: *depositphotos.com/annakhomulo* & *depositphotos.com/annavalerievna1*

http://www.mleeprescott.com/

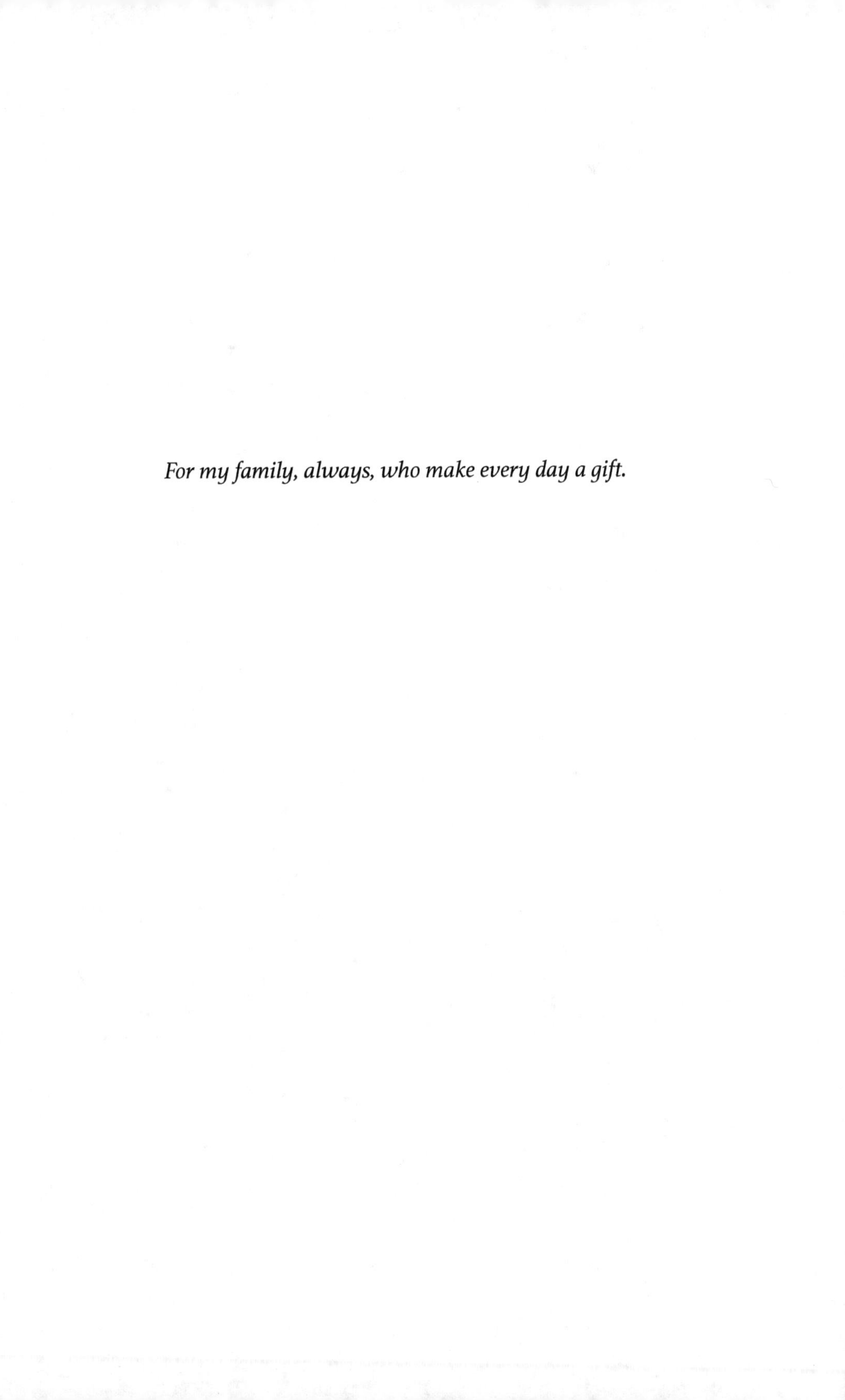

For my family, always, who make every day a gift.

WHO'S WHO IN MORGAN'S FIRE?

Dear readers,

As the Morgan's Fire books continue, many new characters enter the scene. So... I thought it was time to provide you with a characters "Who's Who." Enjoy!

The Darn Yarners

Helen Winthrop
Mavis LaSalle
Rosa Rodriguez
Frankie Brown
Faith Childs Miller
Hope Childs
Grace Childs Straley
Belle Pollart

A group of eight sixty-something women friends who meet regularly and celebrate forty years together in book #4, *Rich's Dilemma.*

1. **Helen Winthrop,** divorced, a stained glass artist. Four daughters, **Lucy, Harriet, Clara,** and **Hazel.**

2. **Mavis LaSalle,** divorced. Owner of Cove Inn and Spa. Four children, **Duncan, Lolly, Dara,** and **Marla.**

3. **Rosa Rodriguez,** married to Cesar. They own the Grille, a restaurant on Main Street. Six children, **Sandy, Raphael, Vincent, Sonia, Michael,** and **Melania.**

4. **Frankie Brown,** divorced private investigator, stained glass artist.

5. **Hope Childs,** single. Owns Cove Yoga Studio.

6. **Faith Childs Miller,** married to **Rex.** Owners of Land's End Farm and Stables. Six children, **Rachel, Rex Jr, Jonas, Brick, Tim,** and **Karen.**

7. **Grace Childs Straley,** widow and director of marine research lab. One child, **Cora.**

8. **Belle Pollart,** manager of docks and fishery with her husband, **Will.** Two kids, **Sadie** and **Billy.**

Morgan's Fire

Richard Morgan, widower, now married to Lucy Winthrop Brennan Morgan. He owns Morgan's Fire Farm, Stables and Vineyard. Eight children, **Rich, Ava, Teddy, Ben, Pam, Gail, Weezie,** and **Wolfie.**

Lucy Winthrop Brennan Morgan, divorced **Dr. Rob Brennan** and remarried to **Richard Morgan.** Two children, **Amy** and **Rob.** Helen Winthrop's eldest daughter.

Rich Morgan, engaged to Karen Miller. Runs Morgan Enterprises. Richard's oldest son.

Ava Morgan Fielding, married to **Dan Fielding**. Both scientists, at the marine research lab. Three children, **Sasha**, **Cameron**, and **Laura**

Gail Morgan Miller, married to Tim Miller, Public Relations Director, Morgan Enterprises, Richard's daughter.

Pam Miller Rodriguez, married to Sandy Rodriguez. A therapist. Richard's daughter.

Louise "Weezie" Morgan, runs pony camps, gives riding lessons. Richard's youngest daughter.

Wolfie Morgan, manager of Morgan's Fire Vineyard. Richard's youngest son.

Callie Richardson, cook and housekeeper.

Gus Casey, the farm manager, married to **Lynn**. Three children, **Dulcie**, **Cal**, and **Sorcha**.

Kiki Bloom, resident vet.

Zeke Ravensbrook, vintner.

Cara Felspar, Zeke's assistant/apprentice.

Sandy Rodriguez, married to **Pam Morgan**. Former owner of Sandy's, a music venue. Newest venture, a farm to table restaurant at Morgan's Fire. Rosa and Cesar's oldest.

Murphy "Murph" O'Neill, Sandy's good friend and assistant. Comanager of Field and Fire.

Parents, **Fiona** and **Murphy Senior.** Siblings, Seamus, Darby, and Murph's twin sister, Aislan, who drowned as a child of six.

Aurora Lake "Rori", comanager, Field and Fire.

Meryl Stockdale, chef at Field and Fire.

Cove Inn and Spa

Lolly Rogers, divorced from Sandy Rodriguez, one daughter, **Maisie,** Mavis's oldest daughter.

Kendall Reese, Mavis's chef.

Village of Horseshoe Crab Cove

Harriet Winthrop Morgan, married to **Kyle Morgan.** A 5th grade teacher at Hampton Meeting School. Helen Winthrop's second oldest daughter.

Kyle Morgan, married to Harriet Winthrop Morgan. Local veterinarian. Nephew of Richard Morgan.

Tim Miller, married to Gail Morgan. Woodworker and lobsterman.

Cooper "Coop" Merrick, local blacksmith and ironworker. Shares workspace with Tim Miller.

Elise Nolan, therapist. Shares office space Pam Morgan.

Greta Jeffers, social worker at Cove High School. Friend of Pam Morgan Rodriguez.

Jack Faulkner, a developer, renovating an old Inn at Barnum's Ledge.

Roland Jenkins, Jack's boss at Compass Properties.

Pete Santoro, Jack's foreman. His crew includes **Ray Solomos, Stavos** and **Greg and Rory,** college kids.

Jay Hallowell, Jack's attorney and good friend.

Joseph "Joe" O'Leary, former priest, exploring social work as his next avocation.

Marla LaSalle, Lolly's sister, with boyfriend Richie Viveiros, musicians, band The Cherry Pickers.

Dr. Rob Brennan, Lucy's ex-husband.

Dr. Chuck Beaman, Rob Brennan's partner and best friend.

Dr. Cynthia Vogt, doctor and associate of Brennan & Beaman.

Dr. Lou Carina, Rich's urologist.

Vincent Rodriguez bartender at the Grille and Witter.

Raphael "Raffi" Rodriguez, an attorney.

Milania "Milly" Rodriguez, a waitress at the Crab Café.

Hank Averill, runs the village general store, son Kevin.

Avery Coggshall, a local plumber.

Paul and Josie Connors, owners of the Crab Café.

CHAPTER 1

Main Street looked magical with its twinkling Christmas lights and wreath-bedecked street lamps laced with snow. Soft puffy flakes covered Joe's hat and jacket, some settling on his eyelashes, blurring his vision. He blinked them away, wondering if he would ever see clearly again.

Two weeks earlier, Joseph O'Leary, priest at St. Mary's by the Sea, had walked away from his life's work. He had loved being a priest. Saying goodbye had been excruciating, but he knew he wanted a different life, a spiritual life, but one that held the possibility of a wife and family. The dream was there, and after two years of struggle, he knew he could not let it go. Tonight, geography was on his mind. He must move out of the parsonage to make way for Father Flynn. He didn't know where life would eventually take him, but Bayport, home to St. Mary's, might be too close right now. Hence his solo walk down the snowy street in Horseshoe Crab Cove. After grabbing a coffee at the Crab Café, he headed to the village's community garden at the far end of Main Street. As he strolled, the soft light from the shops and their festive window displays warmed his heart. *Such a beautiful season*, he thought. *So full of hope and joy.*

He sighed as he passed through the gate into Laura's Community Garden. The raised beds were now covered with straw, ornamental cabbage and hardy spinach poking through their winter blankets. He'd visited the garden before and always found it to be a deeply spiritual place. Walking to the far end, he brushed snow from a teak bench and sat, the quiet surrounding him.

He sipped his coffee in the growing twilight. Gradually, the snow let up and the lights draping garden fences and trees came on. *Maybe I can make a home here*, he mused, *until I decide upon next steps*.

An elderly couple strolled through the front gate and headed for a plot at the garden's south end. They held tight to each other as they shuffled along, finally pausing at a bed that appeared completely bare until the woman reached down, then straightened up with a handful of crimson blooms. She smiled, offering them to her companion, his expression beatific as he stared at the flowers, then bent to kiss her cheek. As Joe watched, he realized that tears clouded his vision and streamed down his cheeks. Brushing them aside, he was surprised to see the couple approaching.

"Good evening," she said. "Lovely night, isn't it? Nathanial, I believe we've found a kindred spirit who loves the winter garden as much we do."

Joe stood, nodding to them. "It is, indeed, a beautiful spot. May I ask what those flowers are that bloom in the snow?"

"Our winter camellias," she said. "My Nathanial's favorite."

Her companion remained silent, a slight smile on his face as his eyes darted about. Joe recognized the misty confusion of dementia and thought how lucky the man was to have such a loving companion. "They're lovely," Joe said.

She adjusted Nathanial's brightly colored scarf and purple wool beret against the cold, then smiled up at Joe. "Do you live in the village?"

"Not yet. I live in Bayport, but I'm considering a move."

"You won't be sorry."

"I expect that's true," Joe said, walking alongside them to the front gate.

"I'm Elizabeth, and this is my husband, Nathanial."

"Joe."

"Well, here we are," she said, indicating a small sedan in the hardware store lot. "Can we offer you a lift?"

"Thanks, but my car's just up the street."

"Well then, good night, Father Joe. I do hope you settle in our tiny piece of heaven. We'll enjoy seeing you around town. Take care."

With those surprising words, she turned and led her husband off, leaving Joe to stare after them. *Small towns.* Of course they'd have attended services at St. Mary's over the years—weddings, funerals, and others. He felt a twinge of guilt for not recognizing them. *Perhaps without their winter clothes, I'd have known them?*

He made his way to the truck, tossing his empty cup into a sidewalk trash bin. *Is that what I want?* he mused, brushing snow from his front windshield. *Loving companionship in my old age? Am I being selfish, abandoning my Lord and my congregation to serve my own needs?*

CHAPTER 2

Stunned, the O'Neills stared at their parish priest of many years. A visiting priest had given the mass that morning because Father Joseph was supposedly on vacation, but when Joe had called and asked if he might stop by, they invited him to dinner.

"Yes, I walked away," Joe said. "I wanted to tell you all first because I consider you to be family. I hope that doesn't sound presumptuous."

"Of course it doesn't, but when?" Fiona MacGregor O'Neill, the family matriarch, stared from the priest to her husband and son, Murph Junior. The latter had brought his fiancée, Greta Jeffers, to dinner.

"I wrote for dispensation six months ago. I wanted to follow process, but they said dispensation could take years, and I didn't want to wait. I'm at peace with my decision."

"Have you preached your last mass, then?"

"I'm afraid so. I wanted to tell the congregation two weeks ago, to say goodbye properly, but I was asked not to do so."

"But why?" Fiona asked, pushing aside her bowl of lamb stew.

His eyes reflected warmth and sadness as he gazed at his old friend. "It's been on my mind for several years. You may remember that I completed a degree in social work a number of years ago? To assist me in my pastoral duties. That work is calling to me. I turned fifty last winter and thought it might be time."

"This is going to sound like pure selfishness," Murph said, "but are you still able to marry us?"

Joe smiled at the young man he'd known for his entire career as a priest. The summer Murph's twin sister, Aislan, died in a tragic drowning accident had tested the priest's faith in its infancy. "I would be honored to marry you, but not in the Catholic church. At least not at St. Mary's," he added, referring to their parish church where he had presided for twenty-four years. "I'm actually standing with Anna Goodspeed, your village pastor, for the Rogers-Faulkner wedding."

Murph nodded. "I heard about that. Their reception is at Field and Fire. Our first wedding."

"So she's not having it at her mother's fancy wedding venue?" Fiona asked, referring to Cove Inn and Spa, the home of Mavis LaSalle, Lolly Rogers's mother, and one of the most sought-after event locations in New England.

Murph shrugged. "I guess they wanted Mavis to enjoy the day and not be stressed running the thing."

Turning back to their guest, Fiona frowned. "Oh, Joseph, what will we do without you?"

"The same thing you've always done. Worship as the good Catholics you are. Father Flynn will be taking my place. I've met him many times. You'll like him."

"Have you plans for the holidays?" Fiona said.

"Not yet, or should I say, they're still formulating."

"Well, you know you're always welcome here. Seamus and Darby both say they'll be home for Christmas. I'll believe that when I see it, but I know they'd love to see you."

The conversation continued over dessert, Fiona's Irish cream cheesecake, after which Joe prepared to depart. "I move out of the parsonage next weekend. Don't suppose you know of any rental properties? I'll store my things temporarily if I can't find something."

Fiona and her husband immediately offered Joe a bedroom, but before he could reply, Murph Junior interrupted. "This is your lucky day. I've moved in with Greta, so my place is free. It's been crazy busy at the restaurant with the holidays approaching, but I was going to start looking for renters after the new year. You're welcome to it for short- or long-term."

Joe looked at Murph and his beautiful fiancée. She nodded, smiling.

"Are you serious?"

"Absolutely! It's yours if you want it."

"I'll take it."

After saying goodbye to his hosts, Joe walked out with Murph and Greta, and the men arranged to meet the next morning at Field and Fire, the restaurant where Murph served as comanager. "We can drive down and look at my place then," the redhead with warm caramel eyes said as he opened his truck door for Greta. Murph owned a duplex at the south end of Horseshoe Crab Cove on the border of the neighboring town of Southport. He lived on one side and rented the other.

As he waved goodbye to the couple, Joe thought about how fortunate he was to have landed in this close knit community where help and support were never far away.

On a cool December morning at Field and Fire, the wind blew off the river. In blue jeans and green Field and Fire T-shirts, chef Meryl Stockdale and comanager Rori Lake were in the main dining room unpacking boxes of new Christmas decorations. "Thanks for the help," thirty-six-year-old Rori said, her auburn hair tied back. "But don't you have stuff to do to prep for tonight?"

Blue eyes sparkling, her sandy-blonde hair held back with a bandana, the forty-two-year-old chef gave her a look. "No worries. I've got my worker bees chopping and prepping. *This* is important. I *love* Christmas and am so excited to see the transformation of these spaces into a winter wonderland. Such cool decorations."

"Pam's department, not mine. She ordered all this. I hope she won't mind if we get started." Rori referred to the wife of owner Sandy Rodriguez, who was in charge of flowers and table arrangements.

"Well, at least we can unpack them. Oh, look at these beautiful garlands!"

As the women continued to explore the boxes, the door opened, and a tall man stepped inside, his dark brown eyes scanning the room. Meryl spied him first and smiled. Handsome, with a lean, athletic build, she guessed him to be slightly older than she, maybe late forties? "Can we help you?"

When he smiled, his craggy features aligned. *Downright gorgeous!* she mused.

"I'm meeting Murph O'Neill here. Is he in?"

Rori wrapped a long garland around her neck like a boa. "Not yet. You're Father O'Leary, aren't you? I remember you from the restaurant opening."

"Good memory," he said, "but it's just Joe. I've had a recent change in vocation."

"You've left the priesthood?" Rori asked, staring at him.

Joe nodded. "Not what I expected to discuss on this fine winter morning, but yes."

"Sorry," Rori said. "I'm kind of a lapsed Catholic, and I've been meaning to get to St. Mary's. That's where you are, or were, right?"

"That's right. Father Flynn will be taking over. He's terrific, and it's a very warm spiritual community."

Joe was aware of the other woman's gaze, her lovely blue eyes considering him with curiosity and perhaps something more? While he'd had close relationships with women parishioners over the years, Joe had always maintained professional distance. Startled, he realized that his vows of celibacy were in his past, but perhaps not in his future. *What is it about this woman?* Finally, he stepped forward, extending his hand. "Joe O'Leary."

"Oh, my bad," Rori said. "I assumed you two had met. This is our extraordinary chef, Meryl Stockdale."

Meryl took his hand, her eyes meeting his. "Pleased to meet you."

He felt heat course through him at her touch.

The front door opened, and Murph stepped in. "Hey, Joe, sorry I'm late!"

Reluctantly, he released her hand. "The pleasure's mine," he said, and turned to his young friend. "Morning. No problem, I've been chatting with your colleagues."

CHAPTER 3

As Joe and Murph headed out, they ran into Pam Morgan laden with more decorations. "Hey, Pam," Murph called, waving. "Need some help?"

Sandy's beautiful wife smiled at them. "I wouldn't say no."

"Not sure if you've met our family friend, Joe O'Leary. Joe, this is Pam Morgan Rodriguez. Pam, Joe."

"Hello," she said, setting her load on the ground and shaking his hand. "Your name just came up this morning. My partner, Elise Nolan, mentioned you'd called."

"Yes, great to meet you, Ms. Rodriguez."

"Pam, please."

"Pam, I asked Ms. Nolan, Elise, if I might sit down with you two when you have a free moment."

She laughed. "Between the craziness over here and my clients, there's not a lot of free moments, but how about lunch? We're both free Friday. I think Elise was going to phone you."

"My phone's in the truck. I'd be happy to meet with you Friday, so I'll check my messages and get back to her."

All three grabbed boxes from the back of Pam's car. After two trips, Murph and Joe said their goodbyes and departed.

"So he's an interesting guy, isn't he?" Rori said, hand on hip, staring at the now-closed front door. "I've never met a defrocked priest before."

Meryl exchanged looks with Pam. "He wasn't defrocked. He left of his own volition. Those are two very different things."

Rori turned to her companions. "He's kind of cute in an academic, Mr. Chips way."

"And probably trying to find his footing in a whole new way of life," Pam said. "Looks like you two have made a good start unpacking here."

Meryl paused. "I hope you don't mind. I love decorating for the holidays and couldn't resist."

Pam smiled. "Absolutely not! I'll take all the help I can get. The more the merrier. Greta's coming by after school today to help, and maybe my sisters too."

"Do you have a vision or a plan mapped out?" Rori asked, oohing as she unpacked a box of tree decorations.

"Wishful thinking. That was going to be my task this morning. There'll be a tree in every dining room and garlands all along the wainscoting. I've kind of got an idea for the table arrangements. Teddy and Gerry are coming down Friday for the weekend, and Gerry promised he'd help with those. For now, I've got buckets of white roses and greens in the big produce fridge." Pam's brother Teddy and his partner were both artists who lived not far away in Providence.

Rori nodded. "Glad Gerr's coming. He does have an amazing eye."

Pam nodded. "Yes, he does. So let's unpack everything and organize. Sandy and a couple of the guys are picking up the trees this afternoon."

～

"Looks like the restaurant is a huge success," Joe said as he and Murph drove the short distance to the house.

Murph grinned. "Our success has reached the Bayport grapevine?"

Joe chuckled. "Maybe, but I'm kind of a closet foodie. I read all the food blogs and magazines. The reviews have been terrific."

"Yeah, we've been pretty lucky so far, but then, everything Sandy touches turns to gold. Been like that since high school."

"Doesn't hurt to have a world-class chef," Joe said. "Ms. Stockdale was quite a find."

"You interested?"

"In her cooking, yes. Only time I tried it was at the opening."

Murph turned to give him a look. "I wasn't talking about her cooking. I saw the way the two of you were eying each other."

"Give me a break, Murphy O'Neill. I'm only a few weeks out of a life of celibacy. Women are the furthest thing from my mind right now."

"Uh-huh," Murph said as he turned into his driveway. "Here we are."

They walked the property and house, which Joe declared to be perfect. "I can move out my things to make space for you," Murph said. "Do you have a lot of furniture and belongings?"

They stood in the recently renovated kitchen, and Joe gazed around, realizing as he often did how few possessions he had needed for the past three decades. "Not really. I've been living in furnished homes since my twenties. Just books, papers, clothes, and a few favorite things."

"Then I'm happy to leave everything for now. We're not sure where we're gonna live down the road, but Greta's place is fully furnished. Anything that's in your way, just push aside or box up and throw in the barn. I'll deal with it later."

Joe met his friend's eyes. "I'm very grateful for this."

"After all you've done for our family? I'm glad to do it."

They spied a car pulling into the drive through the kitchen window. "That would be my renters," Murph said. "Gene and Lana LaFlamme. They're terrific tenants. Quiet and never nosey or in your face."

The men greeted the LaFlammes and chatted for several minutes before driving back to Field and Fire to collect Joe's truck.

As they parted company in the drive, Joe shook Murph's hand. "Thanks again. I'm forever in your debt. You might have overheard my conversation with Pam? I'm meeting to pick their brains, to see if there might be room for one more social worker slash counselor in their building. I have quite a bit saved up, but I do want to be useful. In fact, if you need any help around here, give me a call. Believe it or not, I bartended my way through college before seminary."

"Better watch out what you say, or you'll be working full-time before you know it."

Joe laughed. "Hope that's true. I'm thinking that it might be an easier transition if I live in and center my work around Horseshoe Crab Cove instead of Bayport. I did consider moving far away and may still, but for now, while I'm getting my bearings, I'd like to try to make living here work."

"Couldn't be a more supportive community. See ya."

As he drove away, Joe wondered, as he did most waking hours of late, if he'd made the right decision. *And right before the holidays too!*

CHAPTER 4

Hand in hand, Lucy and Richard Morgan walked along the cliff path from their farm, Morgan's Fire, toward the cluster of buildings housing Morgan's Fire Winery and the new Field and Fire restaurant. Occasionally, they stopped to enjoy the view of the river below or the fields and vineyards that stretched for miles to the east and north of their property. During one such pause, Lucy rested her head against his strong shoulder, and her husband bent and kissed her.

"How did I get so lucky?" he said, smiling at her.

"How did *we* get so lucky?" she asked, returning the kiss.

"You've brought so much happiness into my life, my darling. And to think, we'd been living here in this little town for almost a year and hadn't run into each other until we met in Saguaro Valley." Richard referred to the Arizona town, home to his older brother Ben and his family. Lucy had traveled west with her mother Helen Winthrop, a friend of the Morgans, and sparks had flown between the then-fifty-year-old widower, father of eight and billionaire businessman, and the thirty-nine-year-old recent divorcee, mother of two and owner of a successful mail-order book business.

She snuggled against him as the breeze picked up, drawing

strength from his warmth. "You wouldn't have wanted to meet me earlier. I was a bit of a mess."

He pulled her into his arms, capturing her lips in a deep, sensuous kiss, his tongue circling hers in the dance they knew so well. "Not any more, though?" he asked as he trailed kisses down her slender neck, hands cupping her breasts, teasing her nipples to ripe, hard buds of sensation.

Lucy sighed, powerless. As she opened herself to him, she felt him grow hard against her belly and began rubbing against him, undulating waves of pleasure coursing through her. "I love you," she said, voice husky.

Richard gazed down at her, his dark-brown eyes sparkling with mischief. "You up for a roll in the hay?"

"Ticks?"

He arched one bushy eyebrow, grinning. "That's what glasses, magnifying glasses, and loving spouses are for. I'll check you if you check me. But, if we're too old for it...?"

"Ha-ha. Don't play the age game with me, buddy," she said, scanning the nearby field. "I see just the spot. Come on!"

He swept her in his arms, stepping several yards to reach a small clear patch where the tall grass parted. "You know, if anyone comes along, they'll see us, my wanton wife."

Lucy chuckled, kissing him. "After our escapade in your study, I think they expect it of us, don't you?"

"You're the most beautiful woman in the world, Lucy Morgan, and I love you with all my heart."

Richard gently set her down, lying beside her. "You wore that skirt for a reason. I see that now," he added as practiced hands lifted the hem of the short denim skirt, slipping her panties off, fingers finding her hot, wet depths.

"Oh baby," he murmured as she unzipped his jeans, hands caressing and stroking the way she knew he loved. "You ready for me."

"Always," she said, guiding him in, her long legs wrapping around his strong back.

"Oh my love," he whispered, joining her in the rhythm they knew so well. Their surroundings disappeared as the couple moved in tandem, deeper and deeper, more and more insistent until they reached an explosive, simultaneous climax that, for some inexplicable reason, left them both laughing.

"Gee, that felt good," he said, kissing her.

Lucy kissed his shoulder, his shirt half off in the frenzy of undressing. "We're crazy. You know that?"

"Crazy in love, baby," he growled, rolling them to their sides. "What do ya say? How was the hay?"

She smiled, kissing him deeply, her fingers running through his thick salt-and-pepper hair. "You look like you've been on a hay ride."

"That I have," he said, drawing her nearer. "Wanna go again?"

"Always, but not here, my love." With a peck on his nose, she drew back. "Come on, tiger. Let's pull ourselves together."

Gently, they brushed each other off and smoothed rumpled clothes. "Here you go, sweetie," he said, retrieving her panties from under them.

As Lucy stood, adjusting her skirt and buttoning her blouse, she looked him over. "They're going to know just what we've been doing, aren't they?"

Laughing, Richard took her hand. "Yup, and I couldn't care less."

As they approached the beautiful building that was Field and Fire, they spied Sandy and Murph in the drive. "Hey, guys," Richard called, winking at Lucy as they neared his son-in-law and his business partner.

"Hey, yourself," Sandy said, eyeing them, but making no reference to their appearance.

"We're coming to check on Friday."

"Menu's set, Meryl's working with Callie. They're cool." They'd reserved the small south private dining room for the joint birthday party celebrating Gail Morgan Miller's thirtieth and Gerry Winters, Teddy Morgan's partner's, fortieth. The restaurant's chef was collaborating with Richard and Lucy's housekeeper and cook, Callie

Richardson, on the menu that included some of Gail and Gerry's favorites.

"What about the bar?" Richard asked. "I'd like it if we could set one up in the room, if possible."

"We're workin' on that," his son-in-law said. "Two of our bartenders are away right now and Friday nights are busy. We're fully booked from four thirty till ten."

"I have an idea," Murph said. "You know Joe O'Leary, right?"

"The priest from St. Mary's?" his boss said as the three stared at him.

"Former priest. He's retired, so to speak, and is looking for work. He was just telling me that he bartended his way through college."

Richard shrugged. "Sounds fine to me if he's game. In fact, if he's free, why don't you and Greta come to dinner tonight and bring him along?"

Murphy shook his head. "I can't. This is Rori's night off, and Sandy's with you guys. I'll give Joe a ring, though."

"We'd still like to have him and Greta tonight. It's a small group, not too intimidating."

"Let me check," Murph said, stepping away from the others to make the call. A few minutes later, he returned with, "He's in. What time?"

"Six?" Lucy said. "But we always have a cocktail hour. Callie should be serving around seven. Tell them to come anytime."

"I'll have Greta call him and coordinate. Thanks," Murph said, marveling as he always did at Richard Morgan's warm hospitality.

The four spent a few minutes chatting about other items, then Lucy and Richard headed to the winery to say hello to his son. When they arrived at the tasting barn, they found Wolfie giving a presentation, so they waved and departed.

As the couple strolled back toward Morgan's Fire arm in arm, he said, "We could stop at our spot."

Lucy smiled, meeting his eyes. "Or we could head home for shower and tick check. Who knows where that could lead?"

Richard kissed the top of her head. "I'm in, my sweet girl. Should we walk a bit faster?"

CHAPTER 5

"What a beautiful spot," Joe said as he sat with Jack Faulkner and his fiancée, Lolly Rogers, on the front porch of their Barnum's Ledge home Tuesday afternoon. All around them, construction was still ongoing. Across the lawn, the newly renovated inn was bedecked with garlands, wreaths, and other holiday trimmings. The couple's cottage sported a large wreath on the front door and candles in each window.

"We love it and can't wait to move in completely," she said, patting Jack's arm.

"So you're fully decorated for Christmas, yet not in residence?" Joe asked.

Jack shook his head, winking at her. "We're here a lot and we've had a couple of sleepovers, but it's too much with all the construction. Besides, for Maisie's sake, we want to wait to move in as a married couple."

Joe smiled. "Ah, yes, the flower girl. Is she around?" He referred to Lolly's seven-year-old daughter.

"School," Lolly said. "She's a very proud second grader."

"I'll bet she is. This whole property is very cool. When's the projected completion date?"

"We're hoping for a grand opening in a couple of months," Jack replied. "The inn should be ready by then and hopefully all or most of the cottages. There's been a slight holdup with wetlands."

Joe sat up. "So, folks, I'm sure you have a million things to do. I don't want to keep you. How can I support you as you prepare for the ceremony?"

"We're in pretty good shape," she said. "My mom's all over it, even though the reception is at Field and Fire, thank God. We've written our vows, and you'll meet us at the chapel tomorrow with Anna, right?"

"Of course. I hope you're at ease with the change in my status," Joe said, gazing from one to the other. "I would, of course, bow out if you'd rather have a practicing priest. Father Flynn, who took over for me, is a wonderful person."

Jack grinned. "You're talking to a lapsed Catholic here. We want *you*. Robbie's looking forward to your big reunion." Jack's older stepbrother Robbie had gone to school with Joe, and the two were dear friends of many years.

Joe smiled. "I am as well. How about you, Lolly? Are you comfortable with the arrangements?"

"Absolutely. Anna's been our pastor for as long as she's lived in the village. Between the two of you, we're in good hands."

They talked for a while longer, and then Joe departed.

"What a great guy," she said as they watched, arm in arm, as Joe's truck pulled out of the drive.

Jack hugged her. "The best. It'll be good for all of us to be together and for Joe to jump right into his new life as a lay pastor or whatever he's calling himself."

"Harriet told Lucy he's thinking of joining Elise Nolan and Pam Morgan's practice as a counselor."

"Nothing stays secret long in this village, does it? What's your plan for the rest of the day?"

"I promised Lucy I'd come back to the office for a few hours to do inventory before all these crazy book events coming up. What were we thinking?"

He pulled her close, kissing her temple. "Like the savvy business women you are, you were thinking about the potential for holiday book fairs and author signings. Wish we were in shape to host something here."

"Next year," she said, turning to kiss him, arms circling his broad shoulders. "Poor you, with such a dowdy, middle-aged bride."

"You'll be the most gorgeous bride this town has ever seen," he said, returning her kiss.

"If everyone promises to wear their rose-colored glasses."

Jack's blue eyes twinkled as he looked down at her. "Never sell yourself short, my darling. You're beautiful, smart, and as sexy as hell. Don't 'spose you have time for a little afternoon delight? How's that for dating myself?"

She smiled, love shining in her eyes. "I thought you'd never ask."

GRETA HOPPED INTO JOE'S TRUCK, HOLDING A BASKET WITH ARTISAN breads. "Thanks for picking me up."

"My pleasure." He gave her a warm smile, marveling as he often did at how lucky Murph was to find her.

"Are you ready for a Morgan dinner? They can be a little overwhelming."

"I'm used to large groups."

Greta laughed. "I guess you are."

"Were we supposed to bring something? I have a bottle of wine, but didn't think of food."

She held up the basket. "Tonight's restaurant order didn't have the extra bread they'd counted on, so I ran into the Moon and Stars on my way home. Kind of like bringing coals to Newcastle, though, as there's always so much food."

"I hear Richard Morgan likes nothing better than a party."

"You have no idea."

"How's work going?"

"Busy. How about you? Have you met with Pam and Elise about their practice?"

"We're having lunch Friday."

"I'm sure they're thrilled at the prospect of you joining them. They're getting busier all the time and are always begging me to leave the high school and come work with them. I'd miss the kids, even the difficult ones."

"And I'm certain they'd miss you."

They drove through the village, chatting about town life and Joe's move to Murph's house. Main Street was a beehive of activity, preparations already underway for the weekend's Holiday Sidewalk Days and Tree Lighting Saturday night.

As they turned in at the gate to Morgan's Fire, the peaks of the farmhouse visible in the distance, he whistled. "This is quite a property, isn't it?"

She nodded. "All five-hundred-plus acres of it."

They parked as another car pulled in next to them. Pam and Sandy hopped out with his daughter, Maisie.

"Hi," the child called.

The five of them strolled together up to the house. As they climbed the porch steps, Kyle and Harriet Morgan appeared from the side yard. Joe didn't know either of them well, or most of the dinner company, but he could see Harriet was distressed.

"Hey, guys," Kyle called, his arm around his slender wife. Dark haired and gorgeous, Kyle was the town veterinarian, his wife a teacher in a Quaker school several towns over.

Greta waved and waited as they approached. "Hi. Harriet, Kyle, do you know Joe O'Leary? He's just moved to town."

"Father O'Leary," she said, stepping forward to shake his hand. "So good to see you."

He gave her a warm smile. "Just Joe now. I've retired from my position at St. Mary's."

"Oh, I hadn't heard."

An awkward moment ensued until the door opened and Richard Morgan appeared, arms open. "Welcome, welcome, everyone! Come on in. Everyone's in the family room."

Instantly, they were swallowed up by Morgans, adults and

children. To their left was the door to the dining room, a long dining table set with colorful linens and pottery. To their right was the family room, a cavernous space that nonetheless felt warm and inviting, fires blazing in stone fireplaces at either end, their mantels decorated with greenery, ornaments, and candles. The room had several seating areas with sectionals and chairs, and one corner area furnished with smaller chairs, bookshelves, and bins of toys. Richard spied Joe gazing around the child-friendly area. "That's my grandchildren's domain."

"Lucky kids."

"We're the lucky ones. So glad you could make it. Welcome to the village, by the way. I hear you're moving into young Murph's?"

Joe nodded. "Word travels fast."

"Small town. Lucy and I will get you over for a quieter meal soon. I understand you're old friends with Jack Faulkner. You may have heard that his fiancée, Lolly, is in business with my very talented wife," Richard said as his spouse came up and slipped her arm around her husband's waist.

"Welcome. We're so pleased you could join us." Her pale-blue eyes were warm as she extended her hand, which Joe took.

"Thanks for having me, although I feel like a bit of an interloper to this family dinner."

"Not a bit of it," Richard said. "You're family too. We couldn't be happier to have you. Here's my birthday girl. Do you know my daughter, Gail, and her husband, Tim?"

A petite young woman with curly auburn hair, hazel eyes, and freckles approached, arm in arm with a tall, swarthy man with dark curly hair, brown eyes, and broad shoulders. "Hello," she said. "We've been hearing about you and your brave life change. This is my husband, Tim."

"The lobsterman and savior of horseshoe crabs," Joe said as he shook their hands. "I've heard about your work for many years."

"Gail is the PR genius behind Morgan Enterprises and now the winery and restaurant," Richard said, his face beaming with pride. "Now, let's get you a drink. I know you're friendly with Pam and my son-in-law. Three more of my offspring are around somewhere." He pointed to the far end of the room, where a handsome, bearded young man, his dark hair pulled back in a ponytail, stood talking to a short, young woman with a stylish pixie and sparkling chocolate eyes, who was waving her hands in the air in an animated conversation. "That's Wolfie, my youngest, and his sister, Weezie. He manages the winery, and she works down at the stables running pony camps and giving lessons. My eldest, Rich, CEO of pretty much everything is here too, probably hiding out."

As Joe followed his gregarious host, he wondered if he'd ever get all the names straight. A beer in hand, he was headed to where Greta stood with Pam when the kitchen door opened and Meryl Stockdale appeared, tray in hand. The door caught her on the elbow, and the tray tipped precariously.

Joe put down his beer and came to her rescue. "Here, let me," he said, steadying the tray with one hand and reaching behind her to hold the door open.

She gazed up at him, a startled look in her eyes. "Oh, thank you." She quickly regained control of the tray of assorted appetizers. "Don't suppose you know where they'd like these?"

Lucy and her sister Harriet stood nearby.

Joe smiled. "No, but our hostess is right there. Shall I ask her?"

CHAPTER 6

Dinner conversation topics ranged from the upcoming village Tree Lighting and Sidewalk Days to the double birthday party Friday night and upcoming village weddings. Flanked by Weezie and Wolfie Morgan with Kyle and Harriet across from him, Joe was content to listen to the family's lively banter. As the meal progressed, he found himself thinking about Field and Fire's lovely chef, who hadn't reappeared after leaving the tray of appetizers. Lost in thought, he was startled when he realized Kyle had spoken to him.

He met the young vet's eyes. "I'm terribly sorry. I was daydreaming."

The other man smiled, his brown eyes warm. "No problem. You must daydream a lot these days in the midst of such a huge life transition."

"No excuse for rudeness. You were saying?"

"Nothing. Just dinner small talk. I remarked that you must be busy with all the upcoming weddings. I hear you're marrying Murph and Greta as well as my sister-in-law's friend and Jack Faulkner."

Joe nodded. "Jack is a friend of many years, and I've been close to Murph and his family since I began at St. Mary's."

When Harriet met his eyes, Joe noticed that her own reflected sadness. "What a sad time that was when Aislan died. Poor Murph and his parents," she said.

Kyle gave his wife a puzzled look.

"Yes, it was my first year as a priest when Murph's twin drowned. A tragic accident. Did you live in the area then?"

"Only a few years," she said. "My mom brought us here, to what had been a summer house, after my parents separated. I remember hearing about it. I think our mother and her group of friends reached out to Murph's mother."

Joe smiled. "The Darn Yarners. I've heard so much about them over the years."

"Yes, they literally saved my mother's life and helped raise us too, especially Frankie Brown. Do you know her?"

"No, a few months ago when I was contemplating leaving St. Mary's, I looked at a house next to Ms. Brown's, but I understand another renter came along."

Wolfie had been listening and turned to him. "Meryl Stockman, Field and Fire's chef."

"Really?"

"Yup. Are you still looking for a place, then?" the dark-haired winery manager asked.

"As it happens, I'm moving into Murphy's house, so I'm all set."

AFTER DINNER, GUESTS MILLED AROUND WITH COFFEE AND DRINKS. JOE wandered from room to room, observing the interactions of what was clearly a loving family. Greta sat chatting with Pam, and as he passed, she raised a finger indicating she would be ready to go soon. Kyle had been called out to a veterinary emergency, and they'd offered Harriet a ride home. Joe spied Harriet sitting alone on one of sectional sofas, so he came and sat beside her.

She gave him a wan smile. "A bit overwhelming, isn't it?"

"Your sister and brother-in-law are wonderful hosts."

"Yes, but these large gatherings can be draining for us introverts. I probably should have gone with Kyle."

"I just got the signal from Greta. We should be ready to go soon."

Joe noticed that her eyes were rimmed with tears. "Are you okay, Ms. Morgan?"

She brushed a tear from her cheek. "Not really."

"I know we're recent acquaintances, but I'm a pretty good listener and very discreet. Can I help?"

"I'm forty-one, almost forty-two, and I'm pregnant."

"And this isn't a happy state?"

"I'm miles too old. Kyle's over the moon, but I'm scared to death. My husband's nine years younger, you see."

"Your age difference isn't apparent," Joe said. "Given my life of celibacy, I'm no expert on babies, but I've baptized many babies whose mothers were well into their forties."

"I know it's possible, but I never thought... I mean I'd given up hope of children many years ago."

"Have you seen a doctor?"

"Not yet. I just found out today. I took a test."

"Then that might be a good first step?"

She nodded, drying her eyes. "Yes, you're right. I'm planning to make an appointment in the morning."

"Good," he said, reaching over to touch her hand.

"Father O'Leary... I mean Joe, I haven't told anyone. Not even my mom or sisters. I've asked Kyle not to say anything either."

Joe squeezed her hand. "No worries. Your news is safe. Ah, here comes our fellow traveler," he said, as Greta approached. "Are you ready? I know Harriet and I are."

"Almost. I'll just say goodbye to Lucy and Richard," Greta said.

All three of them said their goodbyes and headed out to Joe's truck. "I'm sorry," he said as they reached it. "We'll be a little squished. I didn't think when I volunteered."

"No worries," Harriet said, her voice a bit more cheerful now. "I'm used to riding around with a bunch of animals piled in beside me." She hopped into the small rear seat, allowing Greta to sit in front.

"Are you sure?" she asked, gazing back at her.

"Absolutely."

When they reached Harriet and Kyle's cottage at the edge of the Hampton Friends campus, Joe stepped out and held out his hand to her. After she said her goodbyes to Greta, he walked her to the door.

"This is a lovely spot."

"One of the perks of teaching at Hampton Friends. This is a school property. We love it, but may move to the village soon. It would be easier for Kyle and the practice. He gets calls at all hours of day and night."

"Well, goodnight then," he said, extending his hand, which she shook before leaning forward to hug him.

"Thank you for listening. It felt good to tell someone."

"I'm happy I was there." He reached into his pocket and brought out a card. "This isn't current as I'm no longer at the church, but my cell number is on it. Call anytime if I can help."

"Good night, Joe. We're so lucky to have you moving to the village."

"I'm the lucky one," he replied, turning to go as she slipped in the door.

"Everything okay?" Greta asked as he slid back into the truck.

"It's good to be at the right place at the right time, isn't it?" he said, backing out of the drive.

If Greta was puzzled by his enigmatic reply, she gave no indication. "Of course, yes, it is."

When they reached her cottage on the bluffs north of town, Greta grabbed her empty basket and slid out. "I'm fine, no need to walk me to the door. Thanks for the lift."

"My pleasure."

She walked around to his side of the truck, hand resting on the door. "And Joe, thank you so much for agreeing to do our wedding. It means the world to Murph, but I imagine it might be difficult for you right now."

Joe put his hand over hers. "Knowing that I'm playing a small part in the marriage of you and that extraordinary young man is a privilege, my dear. To see him so happy is one of life's miracles. Good night."

He watched as she walked to her door and disappeared, then pulled out of the lane and headed back to Bayport. In a few nights, he would move out of his home of over two decades, a home that came with an avocation from which he had walked away. Like a weighted blanket, sadness pressed down on his shoulders, the ache in his heart palpable.

CHAPTER 7

"Where are you off to?" Richard asked as his fifth child and second-to-oldest daughter rose from the table and filled a thermos from the coffee urn on the buffet. They had just ended their weekly Morgan Enterprises meeting, which ordinarily happened on Mondays, but which they had postponed until Thursday this week. Her brother Rich had already skipped out.

Gail turned to him, a grin on her face. "My dear husband, who I've barely seen in three weeks, is taking me on a drive to Lindels to buy greenery and our tree. The apartment needs some decorating. It will never match this," she said, waving her arms around at their surroundings, which were festooned with greens, garlands, and holiday decorations of all sorts collected over a lifetime of family Christmases. "But we want to give it some holiday cheer."

"These belong to all of you," he said, gesturing at the decorations. "If you see anything you want, please take it home. Lucy has boxes of decorations from her home too."

Gail came around and hugged him. "Thanks, Dad. Faith's offered Miller Christmas décor as well, but we want to start out own traditions."

"Of course you do. I guess this houseful of paraphernalia will be buried with me."

"Don't despair. You've got seven other offspring. I'm sure you can pawn some of it off on them."

"Hmm... There's a thought. Have a good time, sweetie."

As she disappeared, Richard mused at the change in his daughter, whom he had always referred to as his prickly little hedgehog. Much softer now, Gail was more peaceful and miles happier since her marriage to Tim. She had blossomed into a loving partner with a husband she adored and who clearly adored her.

"Penny for your thoughts," Lucy said, poking her head around the door.

"Just thinking how lucky I am," he said, holding out his hand.

Lucy crossed the room and sat on his lap. "Me too. Now, what's still on the to-do list for tomorrow's birthday dinner?"

"Nothing. Between Callie getting all the bedrooms ready and the Field and Fire crew, everything's ready to go."

"When do Gerry and Teddy arrive?"

"About six. They're picking Gerry's mom up at the airport, then heading down."

"I'm so glad Stella could come. I really like her."

"Me too. She's a strong, amazing woman. Had to be from what I've heard about Gerry's dad."

"Too bad Gerry didn't have siblings. They can help get you through the rough patches," she said, nestling into his arms. Her own father had been no picnic, her mother, Helen, the strong one. Lucy ran her fingers through his thick salt-and-pepper hair, kissing him on the forehead. "So... I took the day off from Merlin's Closet, and if we have no party planning to do, what will we do with ourselves?"

"I'm sure we'll think of something," Richard said, drawing her near and kissing her deeply as his hand moved up to caress her breasts.

At that moment, Callie, their housekeeper, stepped in to clear the buffet. "Oh, sorry, folks. I can come back later."

Lucy laughed, standing up and ruffling her husband's hair one last time. "No, Callie! You go right ahead. We're just leaving."

"Uh-huh," the blonde housekeeper said, giving them a knowing smile.

Richard patted his wife's round perfect ass. "Cal knows we're still honeymooners, baby. After the past few years, nothing shocks her. How 'bout we take a ride this morning? If we bundle up, the Loop Trail should be clear enough."

"Perfect idea," she said. "Would you like to join us, Callie?"

"Thanks, but that would spoil the fun should you find a secluded spot along the trail." Grinning, she turned and disappeared into the kitchen, a tray of dishes and cups in her arms.

"I felt badly not telling Dad this morning," Gail said as Tom turned the truck south on the way to Lindels. "My pants are starting to get tight."

Tim reached over and took her hand. "Well, there's no reason why you can't, why we can't, sweetheart. I mean, you're almost five months, and the doctor says the baby's healthy."

"I know... It's just that it's been so nice to have it be our secret. Something we shared that the rest of this small town and our two big nosey families didn't know about."

"Well, maybe tomorrow night's the night? What do you say?"

"I hate to take the focus away from Gerry. It's his night too."

His dark-brown eyes shone with love as he looked over at her. "Think about it. Maybe it's time to tell the world?"

"Maybe it is," she said, leaning over to rest her head on his shoulder.

CHAPTER 8

The restaurant kitchen buzzed as Meryl and her staff prepared for a fully booked Friday night as well as the private birthday party in the south dining room. The birthday dinner was a collaborative effort between Field and Fire and Callie Richardson. The Morgans' housekeeper had prepared the broccoli-and-watercress soup, one of Gail's favorites, and the restaurant the lobster bisque, a light creamy version of the classic soup already famous throughout the area. Meryl's bisque was the most requested takeout item, and they prepared gallons of it every day.

Callie prepared the rack of lamb, another dish Gail had requested and Meryl, the striped sea bass with fennel, Gerry's request. The guests of honor had given the cooks carte blanche on the side dishes, so they had each prepared several, Callie a gratinee of cauliflower and a pear-and-parsnip puree, Meryl a creamy fennel puree to accompany the sea bass as well as her signature arugula-and-field-greens salad. Callie prepared a gigantic version of Gail's favorite chocolate hazelnut cake, and the restaurant was creating a number of angel food cakes with a variety of sauces—bittersweet chocolate, caramel walnut and strawberry—all following Gerry's mother's recipes.

"Only for my boss," Meryl said, storing the last of the angel food cake sauces in the back refrigerator. "There's a reason why not many restaurants serve angel food cake. They had to pick a dessert that's best prepared shortly before serving." She eyed her sous chef and his assistant. "And I'm putting you two on egg white beating duty at four. Cakes'll go in right after." Meryl tucked a strand of her sandy hair under her Field and Fire bandana, surveying the cavernous, gleaming space. Field and Fire was the best place she'd ever worked, except on nights like this one. Kicking herself for not insisting they hire extra staff for the evening, she looked over as the double doors from the restaurant side opened and Joe stepped in.

"Hi, sorry to disturb. I'm looking for Murph?"

Oh my, he is handsome, she thought, whipping the bandana from her head and running fingers through her hair. "Oh hello. Did you ask Rori?"

"She doesn't appear to be around either," he said, smiling.

"Well... They're probably... I would guess—"

"Boss, I think they went over to the winery," her sous chef, Andy, said.

Meryl nodded, straightening up and adjusting her apron. "Ah, yes. That's exactly where they are, checking all the wines for the night. Can we help you?"

"I'm moving into Murph's place today and wanted to pick up a key. I can wait outside so I don't disturb you."

Meryl waved her hand. "No worries. We're in good shape. I hear you're bartending for the party tonight? Let me show you the setup."

Without waiting for a response, she whisked by him, his scent of woods and citrus almost intoxicating. *Control yourself, Meryl Stockdale! You're not ready to be involved with anyone, least of all a retired priest.*

Joe followed her through the main dining space to the southern end of the building. She swung open French doors to reveal the beautiful, intimate space designed for no more than fifty diners. Holiday greenery and red, gold, and silver decorations adorned the room with its paneled white walls and eastern wall of windows that looked out on the fields and river. On the north wall, there was a small bar with four stools, their legs fashioned from twisting, bleached tree trunks.

Seeing his gaze, she said, "Those are Tim Miller originals, commissioned for the restaurant. There are a bunch of them along the main bar. Cool, aren't they?"

"Extraordinary. He's very talented."

"Yes, he is. Here's your space. I think they've fully stocked the bar, but the fridge is small, so you may have to restock as the evening progresses. You should have plenty of ice, glasses and all, but check with Murph if you need anything."

Joe brushed against her as he stepped behind the bar. "Oh, pardon me."

Meryl blushed. "No problem."

After a quick survey, he said, "I think I can handle it. I'm a bit rusty and not sure about some of the new cocktails, but I'll google them after I get settled at Murph's."

Meryl laughed. "Come on. I'm sure I can find you a mixology book or two behind the main bar."

As they exited the room, they found comanagers, Murph and Rori sitting at a table, chatting. "Hey, Joe," he called, waving him over. "Have you met Rori?"

Joe approached, smiling at his colleague. "Yes, nice to see you again." He turned to Murph. "I can see you're really busy, so I won't disturb you. Just wanted to pick up the key to your place."

"Absolutely. Keys are in the office. Come on back."

Joe nodded to Rori and followed Murph into a small, cluttered office with four desks, one in each corner. "Here you go," Murph said, sliding a key from his key chain. "There's also a key under the turtle beside the back door, if you forget or lose this one."

"Thanks, Murph," he said, smiling at the younger man.

"Need anything else?"

"Nope, I'm good."

"So I guess you and Meryl are getting along."

Joe grinned, giving him the eye. "She was showing me the bar setup."

"'Course she was."

"I'll let *you* get back to work, Murphy O'Neill."

"See you back around five?"

"Yup. Any special dress code?"

"Nice pants and I'll grab you a Field and Fire T-shirt. We're pretty casual for the waitstaff and bartenders."

Murph opened a closet and surveyed stacks of sage-green T-shirts. "Extra-large I'm guessing?"

"Probably best."

As they parted company near the front door, Meryl approached, holding two slender books. "Here you go. These should help you brush up. When in doubt, ask the customer. Chances are they'll be able to tell you exactly how to make their drinks."

He grinned, taking them, their fingers touching for a second. "Good tip, and thanks for the tour."

"My pleasure," she said. "See you tonight." With those words, she hurried away, not wanting the others to see her red face and trembling hands. *Oh boy, the man is sexy as hell!*

CHAPTER 9

FOR

A Birthday Celebration
for
Gail Morgan Miller and Gerry Winters
Menu
Broccoli Watercress Soup or Lobster Bisque
Parslied Rack of Lamb
or
Baked Striped Bass with Fennel
Gratinée of Cauliflower
Pear and Parsnip Puree
Creamy Fennel Puree
Chocolate Hazelnut Cake
Angel Food Cake with a Variety of Sauces (bittersweet chocolate,
strawberries, caramel walnut)

Sandy and Murph stood surveying the room as waitstaff cleared dinner plates. "Well, we did it, buddy," Sandy said, clapping his hand on his best friend's shoulder.

"The meal was pretty spectacular, wasn't it?" Murph said. "Everything seems to be running smoothly in the restaurant too. Meryl and her gang have outdone themselves."

A few guests gathered at the small bar, and children skipped around the edge of the room or gazed out the windows, sticky hands leaving handprints along the clear surface.

"Remind me to put window washing on the cleaning crew's list," Murph said.

"Cute bunch of rascals, huh? Who would've thunk it two years ago, man. No more Sandy's, I'm married, and you're about to be, and now this."

"We're pretty damn lucky, aren't we?" Murph said, winking at Greta, who sat nearby. "Before we lapse into total nostalgia, I'd better check on Joe and see if he needs anything."

"He's done great tonight. Does he need extra work? We can always use him."

"I think he's still figuring out his next steps, so maybe. He certainly has a bartender's listening skills."

Sandy held his friend's arm. "Hey, before you go, what's the plan for dessert?"

"Waiters'll bring the cakes in a few minutes. Also bowls of ice cream. After the singing, they'll take orders and serve, then leave the cakes and all on the buffet near the coffee setup."

"Perfect."

As Murph neared the bar, Rex and Brick Miller, Tim's brothers, grabbed their drinks as they thanked Joe. "Great party, man," Brick said. "Sorry our kids are getting a little out of control. I'll set these down and corral them."

Murph laughed. "A, it's not my party, and B, I don't think anyone cares what that gang of hellions is doing. This is a kid-friendly zone." As the brothers walked off, he turned to Joe. "How's it going?"

"Okay, I think," Joe said, smiling at him. "I've got my mixology books hidden back here in case I get stuck, but it's been pretty easy. Mostly wine and beer with a couple of cosmos and Bloody Marys."

"You running low on anything?"

"Beer needed restocking, but one of the kids did that, so all set, I think."

"Bar'll stay open for after-dinner drinks until we call it a night,"

Murph said, sitting on one of the barstools. "You're getting rave reviews, you know. This could be your new career."

Joe laughed. "Tempting, but probably not. If you ever get stuck, though, feel free to ask."

"It's your personality. Anyone can serve drinks."

"Flattery will get you nowhere," Joe said as the doors opened and Meryl and Callie appeared, followed by three waiters with bowls and trays. The chef held a large tray with three towering angel food cakes and Callie another tray with an enormous, multilayered chocolate cake. All the cakes were ablaze with candles. As everyone burst into "Happy Birthday," Meryl set her cakes in front of Gerry and Callie placed the beautiful tiered cake before Gail.

As the singing died down, Gerry eyed his cakes and chuckled. "This is not a one-man job! I definitely need reinforcements to blow out all these candles."

"Me too," Gail said.

"Make a wish, everyone," Richard called out as children and adults gathered round the cakes. "One, two, three!"

As Callie and Meryl moved the cakes to the buffet, Richard announced that waitstaff would be taking dessert orders. Once everyone was served, the toasts began.

Stella Winters, Gerry's mom, gave a touching tribute to her son and the love of his life, telling them all that the day he met Teddy, "My baby's life was changed forever." She thanked the Morgans for their hospitality and sat down with tears in her eyes.

Richard gave a similar toast and thanked everyone for coming. He ended with, "I would be remiss if I did not thank our dear Callie, the talented Meryl Stockdale, my son-in-law, Sandy, and his entire staff for the incredible food and service, including our terrific bartender for the night, Joe O'Leary. Bravo to all!"

Gerry then stood with Teddy at his side. "Thanks, everyone. We love you all. And we also have an announcement, really two announcements. I'll defer to my partner to do the honors."

The second Morgan brother rose, brushing a lock of sandy hair from his eyes. He cleared his throat and gazed around the room before speaking. "I was expecting Gerry to share our news, so this is a bit of a surprise. As you all know, we've been engaged for as long as we've been together, but now we've finally decided to make things legal. I know how much our dad loves a party, so he and Stella are the only ones who've heard this. We've finally set a wedding date of April seventeenth of next year, here at the farm. We'll pray for a good day, but Dad's had heat installed in the barn, and as we all know, he's got tents and heaters for them too."

A cheer went up from the crowd, punctuated with comments like "It's about time" as Teddy waited, scanning the room. He was holding Gerry's hand when the room finally quieted. "Our other news is... Well, we're very pleased to share that we're going to be parents. Our baby will be born this coming June, to a surrogate mom. She's a dear friend, she's bright, warm, amazing, and in the bloom of health. Almost two months along now."

More cheers rang out as Richard came around the table to hug his son and Gerry, clapping both of them on the back. He then stepped back to cede the space to Stella. As a number of people rose to congratulate the couple, Gail turned to Tim. "After that, our announcement will seem a bit anticlimactic."

He kissed her forehead, his eyes filled with love. "No, it won't. Let's give 'em a couple of minutes to settle down."

After most people had returned to their seats with more cake, coffee, or aperitifs, Tim Miller stood up and tapped the side of his beer bottle with a spoon. As all eyes turned to him, he surveyed the crowd, a grin on his handsome face. "Okay, folks, the birthday girl would like to say a few words."

Blushing crimson, Gail stood and slipped her arm around his waist. "Oh no, you don't. You're staying right by my side." Almost a foot taller than his wife, Tim circled his arm around her shoulders, drawing her close.

"Those of you who know me well know that even though I'm a PR person, I personally am very attention averse. However, I do want to thank everyone for this lovely party. It's meant so much to me. To have us all together and to share this special night with Gerry have been rare and precious gifts." She paused, looking up at Tim before continuing.

"You've got this, baby," he whispered.

Turning back to her family and friends, Gail said, "I... We also wanted to share our news. It turns out that there's mini baby boom going on in our family. By the time of Teddy and Gerry's wedding, we will either have a new baby or I'll be waddling around nine months pregnant."

More cheers and many congratulations followed by hugs and kisses for the couple ensued. As this was going on, Joe looked over and spied Harriet and Kyle. He had his arm around her, and she was shaking her head. He didn't have to guess at topic of their conversation. He wanted to add to the baby boom news, and she clearly did not.

Joe stepped from behind the bar and headed their way. When he reached their table, he stood behind Harriet's chair and said nothing, but gently put his hand on her shoulder.

This tableau did not escape Lucy's notice. Immediately, she stood up and made her way toward her sister. Something was bothering Harriet, and she suspected the kind ex-priest knew what it was.

CHAPTER 10

Twilight had already given way to darkness at five fifteen Saturday afternoon, when Joe parked next to Laura's Garden, its twinkling lights casting a soft glow on the beautiful green space. He grabbed scarf, hat, and gloves from the passenger seat and hopped out of the truck. Christmas in the village was magical, all the shop windows on the north side of the street ablaze with lights and greens, reds, silver and gold, each sporting a uniquely decorated tree just outside the door. Wreaths hung from the street lights and an enormous Douglas fir stood in the center of the small green on the south side of Main Street. Vendors selling crafts, decorations, and food ringed the open space, their festive booths lighting up the night.

A light snow fell as Joe walked down the street. As he passed the Café, Harriet stepped out, an oversized cardboard tray with a dozen hot chocolates in her hands. Brown paper bags hung from each arm. "Hello, Ms. Morgan," he said. "Can I help with all that?"

She smiled. "It's for the crew setting up the tree lighting, including my husband. When I left, the Café hadn't set up their coffee station. In fifteen minutes this trip would have been unnecessary."

"Gotta keep the troops happy," he said, reaching out for the wobbly tray. "Allow me. Can I carry one of the bags too?"

"Thanks, but I've got 'em. They're not heavy."

"How are you?" he asked as they headed for the green.

"Better. I told my sister last night. It's feeling more real now."

"I'm glad."

"I didn't get to ask. How did your meeting with Pam and Elise Nolan go?"

"Very well. I'll begin slowly, see a few clients, and see how things go. It's a wonderful space, and they think the accountant downstairs might even have an extra room for me. He owns the building, I guess."

"Yes, Andy Roby. He's a nice man. Well here we are," she said as they neared the group working on the green. "Is this the first time you've been to our tree lighting?"

"Yes. St. Mary's always hosted their own. It's tomorrow this year."

"Will you go?"

"I haven't decided. Might be easier for Father Flynn and my former parishioners if I didn't. There are still hurt feelings, and I'd hate to stir them up on such a happy occasion."

"Our savior!" Kyle said, meeting them and taking the bags from his wife's arm, kissing her cheek. "Thanks, darling. I see you found reinforcements."

"Yes, Joe was very kind."

"Evening," Joe said. "Where would you like these?"

Kyle pointed to a picnic table. "Over there would be great. We're about finished with everything, so it's a good time to take a break. You warm enough, baby?" he asked, gazing at her.

"Perfect. You go. I'll get an ornament for both of us and hang them on the tree. Thanks, Joe," she said as she headed for another table holding baskets of simple wooden ornaments, markers, and ribbons. It was a village tradition to decorate an ornament, write a simple wish on its back, thread one of the brightly colored ribbons through its top, and hang it on the community tree among the bright baubles and lights already adorning it. A red ladder and several elves stood nearby in case anyone wanted their ornament hung high in the magnificent branches.

"Hey, Joe!" Murph called as a group from Field and Fire walked onto the green. His comanager, Rori, walked beside him, and a number of the waitstaff, bartenders, and kitchen staff trailed behind. Joe spied Meryl at the rear of the group, walking with Greta.

Joe walked over to greet them. "Evening. You all must have timed your entrance just right."

"We borrowed the winery van. The restaurant has a delayed opening tonight so we could come for the lighting. How're you settling in?"

"Only been one night, but I like it. Very quiet except for the coyotes howling."

"Yeah, I forgot to mention that. They're quieter in winter, but some nights, they do seem to perk up."

As Joe gazed around at the gathering crowd, he spied a large contingent from Morgan's Fire, including stable hands and the household, Lucy and Richard walking with Callie, Pam, and Sandy. He turned back to Murph. "That was kind of you all to open Field and Fire later so the young people can experience this."

Murph laughed. "Have you met my boss? Most generous guy in the world, and he loves this as much as we do."

"Looks like the whole village is here."

"Pretty much."

"Hi, Joe," Greta said, coming to stand beside her fiancé, slipping her arm around his waist, Meryl right behind her.

"Hi, ladies," he said, nodding to Meryl, then turning to Greta. "How's that little goat of yours doing? I forgot to ask the other night."

"She's as good as gold, and she loves Murph. I'm afraid she prefers him to me."

"Does not," Murph said, draping his arm around her shoulder. "Daisy is my second girlfriend, though. There's a booth selling dog collars, babe. Want to go check it out? I bet they'd fit the Daise."

Joe turned to Meryl, who looked like a Nordic snow princess, her red wool cap and green down jacket sprinkled with white. She wore a long, colorful scarf around her neck, the swirling greens and blues bringing out the blue in her eyes. She had the most beautiful eyes he'd ever seen.

"We're both experiencing our first Horseshoe Crab Cove tree lighting, I guess," he said.

"But you've lived here for years."

He smiled. "Bayport's another world. The parish has its own ceremony."

"Well, we'll enjoy it together, then," she said, her lips beginning to tremble.

"You're cold. I have a couple of blankets and fleece things in the truck. Can I run and grab you one?"

"Thanks, but maybe some hot chocolate will warm me up. We're not here for too long."

"My treat," he said as they began walking toward the coffee cart, a line already formed for hot beverages and doughnuts.

As they reached the line, he spied a booth selling handmade scarfs, shawls, and other woven items. "You keep our place in line, and I'll be right back."

He searched briefly and selected a twin-size blanket in a woven pattern that reminded him of the colors of the ocean. When he returned, Meryl stood shivering, almost at the front of the line. "Here you go," he said, slipping the blanket around her shoulders.

She looked up at him, her eyes registering surprise. "But I can't—"

"I need an extra blanket at Murph's, so I thought why not?" he said. "Unless you'd like it for your house?"

"I don't, and I couldn't accept it anyway, but thank you for the loan. It feels wonderful."

"Good. My mother was a weaver, so I thought that kind of Shetland wool and that tight weave would be warm."

Her eyes softened as they met his. "That was very kind of you."

Joe smiled back, surprised by his feelings of protectiveness toward this woman he barely knew. "It suits you. The colors."

At that moment, they were interrupted by a voice asking, "What can I get you folks?"

They both ordered hot chocolates and took them to stroll the booths, saying hellos to a number of people along the way. Like old friends who'd known each other for years, they walked in companionable silence or engaged in familiar conversation, each acutely aware of the other beside them.

"Do you know about the ornament tradition?" he asked as they neared the tree.

"One of the kids was telling me about it on the way over."

"Shall we?" Joe gestured to the table with markers, ribbons, and piles of wooden ornaments in various shapes.

Ornaments and markers in hand, they were headed for a bench nearby when Joe heard someone call his name. "Hello, Father Joe!"

He turned to find the elderly couple from the garden, Elizabeth and Nathanial. She held his arm, guiding him forward.

"Good evening. It's just Joe now. How are you both?"

"Very well and enjoying the holidays, aren't we, Nathanial?" Her husband nodded, his confused eyes darting from one to the other of them.

Remembering his manners, Joe said, "This is my friend Meryl. Do you all know each other?"

"We don't," Meryl said, stepping forward to shake first Elizabeth's, then Nathanial's gloved hands. "Pleased to meet you."

"Our pleasure, dear. Are you new to the village as well?"

"Fairly new. I'm the chef at Field and Fire."

"How thrilling to make your acquaintance. When my daughter comes next month, she's promised to take us there. We hear wonderful things about your cooking."

"How kind of you to say."

Joe observed the couple, all bundled in coats, scarfs, hats, and mittens, then reached into his pocket. "This is my card. I'm working in town and living ten minutes down the road in Southport. I would be honored to take you to Field and Fire some evening."

"Aren't you a dear man," Elizabeth said, patting his arm with her mittened hand. "Nancy made us promise to wait till she arrives to try it, but you never know. If we like it, we might just call you in February to be our chauffer. I don't drive at night anymore."

"How did you get here tonight?"

"We live just down the street past the garden. The house next to that beautiful old Victorian."

"Which just so happens to be where my new office will be. Part-time social worker."

"So we're to be neighbors with Joe. Nathanial, did you hear that? Now, I see you haven't hung your ornaments, so we're going to let you decorate them. My sweetheart and I just hung ours. Very nice to meet you, dear," she said, smiling as she gave Meryl a slight bow.

"You too. I'll look forward to seeing you around town and at Field and Fire."

"Night, you dear, sweet man," Elizabeth said, smiling as her warm eyes met Joe's. Then she took hold of her husband's arm, winking as she turned away. "Enjoy your evening," she said as they vanished into the crowd.

"What a sweet couple. He has dementia, doesn't he?"

"Something like that. We've only met once before, in the garden. There's something almost magical about them, isn't there?"

Meryl smiled. "I think you may be right. Now, come on, we'd better color our ornaments, make a wish, and get them on the tree before the lighting."

Joe made a mock bow. "Lead the way, milady."

Meryl had chosen a bell and a candy cane. After adorning the front, they turned each piece over to write a wish. Meryl wished for a sense of belonging, and Joe, peace and balance in his own life and the world.

"I'll get us some ribbon," he said, rising to return the markers to the table and selecting two strands of precut red ribbon. "Here you go," he said, smiling as he handed her a ribbon.

"Thanks."

Her eyes lingered on his for a few seconds before turning to her task. There was something tangible and precious going on, but Joe couldn't quite identify it. *Is it attraction? Lust? Affection?* After a lifetime of celibacy and alliance to God, he was like an infant feeling his way in an intriguing but alien world.

Each found a place on the tree for their creation. Neither had intended to share their wish, but as they stepped back, she asked, "Care to share your wish?" When he told her, she said, "That's lovely. I just want to belong somewhere. I've moved so much that it would be nice to put down roots."

"I have a feeling this is a place where that could happen."

Behind them, a bell rang, signaling the tree lighting would be soon. Some of Meryl's coworkers joined them, and they all moved together to stand with the crowd circled around the Douglas fir. This year, the town council had asked Mavis LaSalle, Lolly Rogers's mother and owner of the Cove Inn and Spa, to pull the handle and light the tree. This year's honor had gone to the wealthy land owner because of her generosity in donating large tracts of land to the town. She had deeded two parcels for the community garden and had recently donated five acres for new athletic fields.

All eyes turned to the small makeshift stage, where Hank Averill, owner of the general store and head of the town council, stood beside a tall, rail-thin sixty-something woman. Hatless in the bitter cold, her long black hair streaked with gray reminded Joe of Morticia from *The Addams Family*. Even from a distance, her violet eyes sparkled, striking eyes that her daughter had inherited. A member of the Darn Yarners, Mavis was by far the most glamourous and exotic, often seen in the warmer months driving through town in her Mercedes convertible, top down, a long Isadora Duncan-type boa flying behind her.

Hank stepped forward, mike in his hand. "Welcome, folks, to the forty-fifth annual tree lighting. When the village started this tradition, this tree was no more than a sapling. Now it towers above us, majestic and glorious, promising to be here forty-five years from now as well. We're pleased and proud to have one of our most generous citizens, Mavis LaSalle, pull the lever this year. Let's give her a big round of applause."

The crowd erupted with cheers and clapping as the woman came forward, looking like a snow goddess in a long red coat with fur collar, a matching fur hat held in her left hand. "Thank you all for this great honor."

Her right hand grasped the green lever and pushed it downward to light the enormous, glittering tree. Applause and expressions of awe echoed in the beautiful space as people stared upward. Joe gazed over the crowd to where Meryl stood with her colleagues and smiled. Their eyes met for a second before Murph called, "Okay, group, time to get on the bus!" and just like that, she was gone in the crowd that moved and swirled around him.

Joe watched as villagers dispersed, some headed to vehicles, others taking another pass at the booths. "Quite something," Richard Morgan said, coming to stand beside him. "This is my fifth tree lighting, and it's still magic."

"Sure is," Joe replied as Lucy Morgan came to her husband's side.

"Hi, Joe, so nice to see you."

"Same here."

"I'm going to break down our stall," she said, referring to a small booth displaying Merlin's Closet's selection of holiday books. "Don't suppose you two want to lend a hand? We've got Jack and Amy and Rob, but we can always use more helpers."

"Count me in, sweetheart," Richard said, drawing her close for a quick hug.

"Me too," Joe said. "Lead the way."

As he followed the couple to the brightly decorated Merlin's Closet booth, he wondered if he'd ever have a relationship like theirs. He knew a little of the heartache of Lucy's divorce and, of course, the death of Richard's wife, Laura, many years earlier, but weren't they fortunate to have found one another? To an observer, they couldn't be a more loving, happy couple. *Come to think of it, there are many of those around, aren't there?*

CHAPTER 11

Late Wednesday morning, J.J. Faulkner circled the Inn at Barnum's Ledge and parked next to his father's Volvo SUV. A senior at Vassar, J.J. had been named for his father, Jack Jameson Faulkner. No sooner had he stepped out of the car than his dad appeared on the porch.

"Hey, buddy, you're early." Except for his chocolate-brown eyes, people said J.J. was the spitting image of his father, who now came forward, arms wide.

"Decided to beat the traffic, so I left Kennebunk right after a birthday breakfast with Mom. I grabbed a bagel and ran out, much to her dismay."

"Happy birthday. I'm honored to have you here to celebrate." Since his parents' divorce, J.J. had spent every birthday with his mother.

His son grimaced. "Glad to be here."

"How is your mother?"

"Fine. Up to her usual tricks. She and Sheldon are leaving for London tomorrow."

"Of course they are," Jack said.

"Medical conference."

"Uh-huh."

"This place is amazing. Lyddie sent me some photos, but I had no idea. Very cool."

Jack nodded. "It's home now. The Inn opens in the new year, and Lolly and I move in post-honeymoon." At Jack's recommendation, his company, Compass Properties, owned by Roland Jenkins, had bought and renovated Barnum's Ledge. The property consisted of a large three-story inn, several cottages, and smaller outbuildings. All buildings and grounds were in some stage of revival. The company had sold a prime two-acre lot to Jack, and he was now acting as general manager of the resort. He hoped to own it outright in five years.

Father and son carried J.J.'s things up to the cottage. "Are you guys really trusting Lyddie and me not to wreck this incredible house over the weekend with wild parties?"

"Ha-ha. Your sister's in love, hasn't she told you? If she parties at all, I'm predicting it will be a party of two or three, including you."

"When am I meeting the bride?"

"Tonight, if that's okay for her to come to the birthday dinner? There's a terrific restaurant down the coast. Fantastic seafood."

"You don't have to ask, Dad. I'm looking forward to meeting Lolly. I've never seen you looking so well or so happy."

"Things are going really well. I finally found my place after your mother and I split."

"That's terrific. So where is my lovestruck sister?"

"She'll be here in a couple of hours, I think."

"Is her boyfriend coming to dinner?"

"I wanted to check with you."

"Sure, love to meet the Wolfman. That's what they call him, right?" he said as they stepped into the front hall, dining room to the right and a large living room on the water side.

Jack gave him a side-eye. "It's Wolfie."

"So here's the living room. Our bedroom's to the right, through there," he said, leading the way down a short hallway to a light-filled room with cottage-style furnishings painted white and a king-sized bed and a large sitting area with upholstered chairs, the fabrics echoing the colors of the fields and bay outside them. A huge master bath included a soaking tub with magnificent water views. The living room, bedroom, and bathroom all enjoyed the same spectacular, unobstructed views.

J.J. whistled as he stared at the tub. "Wow!"

"Cool, huh?"

His son grinned. "Looks like it's built for two."

Jack grinned. "Build for breathtaking views inside and out."

"All right, Casanova. Lead on. I'm assuming you're not giving me the love nest for the weekend."

Chuckling, Jack led him through the beautiful kitchen with white cabinets, many glass fronted, marble countertops, and gleaming Miele appliances. An eight-foot deacon's table acted as an island in its center.

"Must be nice to be a billionaire," J.J. said, brushing his hand over the table's smooth surface.

"Hardly, but I wanted to do this right. We're pleased. Actually, my future mother-in-law gave us the appliances as a wedding present."

"So she's the billionaire?"

Jack shrugged. "Pretty close, I expect. Come on." He led him through a hall with glass-fronted pantries on either side and opened a door to reveal a tiny staircase, white shiplap paneling lining its walls. "This was an extravagance, but I've always wanted a house with a back staircase."

There were four bedrooms upstairs, each with its own bath. Three of the four had water views, the fourth, a lovely view of the fields to the west. "Take your pick of the first three," Jack said. "The front one is Maisie's, and we haven't furnished it or fixed it up yet. Your sister doesn't care. I asked her."

J.J. poked his head into all three and finally stepped into the one closest to the back stairs, furnished in beach colors and beautiful Shaker style furniture. The view was amazing. "This will do just fine, and I'm close to the kitchen in case I get hungry in the night. There is food, right?"

"Yup. My mother-in-law's chef, Kendall, stocked the fridge and cupboards. She got enough to feed an army."

"You've been to Vermont, huh?" he asked, referring to a furniture maker they loved.

"We have indeed."

"Dad, you've created an incredible home. You-know-who would be salivating if she saw it."

"I'm sure her and Sheldon's place makes this look like a caretaker's cottage."

J.J. laughed. "Sheldon's a minimalist." He took his hanging suitcase from Jack and hung it on the door of the closet, throwing his duffel on the bed. "So let's see what kind of food Kendall's brought in. I'm starved."

JACK HAD REQUESTED THE SMALL DINING ROOM AT THE EAST END OF Bluewater Seafood, which was just the right size for their party of six. Large windows gave a magnificent view of the water, a full moon tracing a shimmering path across the dark bay. "This must be incredible during the daylight," J.J. said, gazing out at the night.

"Those are the lights of Southport down the coast," Wolfie said, pointing.

J.J. had done a bit of research on his sister's boyfriend. Richard Morgan's youngest, the twenty-seven-year-old winery manager sure cut a striking figure on the advertising copy for Morgan's Fire Wines. With long dark hair usually pulled back in a ponytail, Wolfie sported a thick, dark beard, his coal-black eyes piercing. Lyddie sat beside him, hanging on every word. *My little sis is clearly smitten,* J.J. thought, watching them.

Their father had ordered a bunch of appetizers for the table, and they all had drinks in hand. Lolly's daughter, Maisie, sat between her mother and Jack, her chocolate-brown eyes gazing from one adult to the other. The eight-year-old spent much of her time with adults when not in school, so she knew how to behave at a dinner party. As they enjoyed a variety of oysters, little necks, sea scallops ceviche, and shrimp, they discussed what looked good for dinner. Everyone except Maisie chose lobster.

"I can't believe Uncle Joe's living right here in the village," J.J. said. "And he's left the priesthood? What a shocker."

Jack's children had grown up knowing their uncle's friend Joe O'Leary well as they often spent holidays together.

"Yup," Jack said.

"When's Uncle Robbie arriving?" Lyddie asked, popping a littleneck into her mouth.

Jack turned to her as Wolfie draped his arm over his daughter's chair. "They'll be here tomorrow night in time for dinner. He and Davos, along with Nana and Gramps, will be our first guests at the Inn. A few others too. We've hired staff just for this weekend to take care of them and a few other wedding guests." Robbie and his husband, Davos Minori, ran a small, internationally known gallery in Lenox, Massachusetts, started almost forty years earlier by Jack's parents. James and Ester had retired several years earlier in order to travel.

"What about Uncle Jay?" his son asked, referring to Jay Hallowell, Jack's best friend and also his attorney.

"Jay's staying at the Inn, as well as Roland and a couple more from Compass. Pete and the entire crew that worked on this place will be at dinner and maybe stay over. Pete's under strict instructions to keep the crew under control. We don't want the place wrecked before our January opening."

"So what about you, Lolly? Have you got lots of people coming?" Lyddie asked.

Her father's fiancée laughed, her violet eyes shining. Their unusual color was accentuated by the swirling colors of her dress that hugged her ample breasts, revealing a hint of cleavage. Lolly fretted constantly about being dumpy, but it truth, she was a woman who turned heads wherever she went. "You been around long enough to know that most of the village will be there. Jen, my mom's ward and a dear member of our family, is coming too."

Mavis had taken in Jen Honeywell and her brother when her good friends the Honeywells had been killed in a light plane crash. Both had been teenagers at the time, and Jen and Lolly had gone through high school together and were dear friends. Jen taught literature at nearby Clifton College.

"You're kidding," J.J. said, looking from her to his dad. "I thought you said small and intimate?"

Jack chuckled. "There's small and intimate, and then there's Horseshoe Crab Cove small and intimate. It's all about intermarriages and a group called the Darn Yarners. Can't have one Yarner without them all, and Lolly's mother, Mavis, is a Yarner."

"As is my stepmother's mom," Wolfie said.

Maisie sat up straight. "And my grandma Rosa."

"My ex Sandy's mom," Lolly explained, "and Sandy, my ex and Maisie's dad, is married to Pam Morgan. Pam's dad, Richard, is married to Lucy. She's my best friend and business partner. There are eight Morgan offspring, including Wolfie here," she said, smiling in his direction. "And most of them will be there with families. So it goes on and on."

Wolfie grinned. "Fortunately, Maisie's dad opened Field and Fire, so we can take over the entire restaurant."

"With a world-class winery next door," Jack said, gesturing at Wolfie.

Lyddie smiled at her brother. "See what you've been missing not coming sooner?"

"I'll say," J.J. said. "I'd love a winery tour while I'm here."

"Any time, man," Wolfie said. "I'll be there all day tomorrow."

The food arrived, and everyone gave themselves over to the delicious meal. Lobster bibs were donned, and the sounds of cracking and metal clunking echoed up and down the table as empty shells were discarded into metal bowls lining the middle of the table. Cake awaited them at Barnum's Ledge, so after Jack settled the check, the group headed for the exit. As they passed through the main dining room a voice called, "Hey, Faulkners, Rogerses, and Morgans!"

Jack turned to find Richard and Lucy Morgan and Lucy's sister

Harriet and Kyle. "Good evening. We've just had a birthday dinner for my eldest, J.J. I don't think you've met him?"

J.J. stepped forward as Richard stood. "Please don't get up. Wonderful to meet you all. I'm looking forward to the weekend's celebrations."

Lucy smiled up at him. "We are too."

Lolly circled the table to say hello to her friend and business partner, and Kyle came around to shake J.J.'s hand. "Great to meet you. I'm an Arizona Morgan who followed my wife, Harriet, back east."

"Lucky you. You're the vet, right?"

"The very one."

"Well, we won't spoil your dinner," Jack said. "See everyone over the next few days."

"You certainly will," Richard said, sitting back down.

As they exited the restaurant, Wolfie leaned over to J.J. "Don't drive yourself crazy trying to remember who's who. Just nod, smile, and say hey. That's what I did the first year we moved to town."

J.J. laughed. "Good tip."

CHAPTER 12

Friday evening, Mavis entertained the wedding party and out-of-towners at Netherfield Manor. "You ready, buddy?" Jay Hallowell asked Jack. The two men stood side by side in the ornate baroque hall that served as Mavis's formal living room.

"Yup."

"She's the one?"

"You know she is. Doesn't she look gorgeous tonight?" He gazed across the room where Lolly stood chatting with Jen. His fiancée wore a simple crepe dress in cranberry that draped her body perfectly, a delicate gold chain and matching earrings her only jewelry.

"She's amazing, man. Wish I could find someone like her. Her sister's a cutie too."

Jen wore a simple gray sheath and black six-inches heels that showcased her lithe, lovely legs. Her shoulder-length light brown hair was swept back, and she wore silver jewelry that sparkled as she moved.

Jack gave his friend a look. "Jen is like a sister to Lolly, but they're not technically related. She's Mavis's ward and a great person. My advice—don't mess with her. She's got enough on her plate with some Lothario at work."

"Yeah? Maybe I'm the one to break that cycle?"

"Uh-huh."

They were interrupted by Mavis calling everyone to dinner.

AFTER THE BRIDAL PARTY HAD DEPARTED, JOE AND ANNA GOODSPEED, the minister of the village's Congregational Church, sat on wooden pews, chatting. "What you did was very brave," she said, her kind eyes regarding him.

Joe shrugged. "Brave or crazy. I guess time will tell. It's been brewing for a while."

"If I'm not being intrusive, can I ask you why?"

"I'm as devoted to my faith as I've ever been, and I loved my parishioners, but the priesthood no longer felt like my calling. Honestly, I'm still unclear what my calling is. Maybe family and community? Or perhaps it's the possibility of a life partner?"

Anna smiled. "Anyone in mind?"

He hesitated, then said, "No. I wouldn't know what to say or do with a woman."

"So it's been a good life, but you're ready for a change."

"Something like that. You married?"

She chuckled, flipping her ponytail of curly red hair from her shoulder, brown eyes twinkling. "Why? You interested?"

"Oh, I'm sorry. I didn't mean to imply—"

Anna laughed. "No, I'm sorry. I was joking. I've been married almost ten years. He's a painter. Pretty good one too, but of course, I'm prejudiced."

"Would I have seen his work?"

She grinned. "Cove Gallery sells a few now and then, but most of his paintings go to the city—Boston, Providence, and New York."

"And you live in the village?"

"Hampton Meeting," she replied referring to the town twenty minutes north that bore the same name of the Quaker school, Hampton Meeting, where Harriet Morgan lived and worked. "It suits us."

"Well, I'll let you get home to your painter," Joe said, standing and stretching his long legs. "Rehearsal went well. We're ready, don't you think?"

"I do. What a wonderful couple they are."

"The best."

"And you knew his family growing up?"

"Yes, but mostly the brother. He and the parents arrive tomorrow, I understand."

"Well, I'll see you at three tomorrow."

"Night," Joe said, gathering his coat, hat, and tattered briefcase.

"Drive safe. I hear the roads are icy."

"You too." With that, he tipped his hat and turned away into the growing darkness.

"YOU READY, BABE?" JACK ASKED AS HE DREW LOLLY CLOSE. THEY HAD just strapped Maisie into her car seat, and she was already half asleep after J.J.'s birthday cake and ice cream.

"For bed? Yes," she said, smiling up at him. "And for tomorrow. I hope we didn't jinx things by seeing each other tonight."

"Since we're not in a Regency romance, I think we're safe."

"Regency romance? What do you know about them? Is this something I should know about you, hmm?"

"My grandmother loved them, and when I stayed with her, those were the only books on the shelves at her summer house."

"Uh-huh." Lolly's arms circled his broad shoulders, her fingers ruffling his hair.

"I'll see if I can remember some of the plots for the honeymoon."

"Can't wait. Your kids are terrific, by the way."

"Well, you've yet to meet the folks and Robbie, so hold on to your hat."

"I'm looking forward to it. See you tomorrow."

After the short drive from Netherfield to her cottage on the grounds of Cove Inn and Spa, he parked in the drive. He hurried around to open her door. Then, taking her in his arms, he captured her full, luscious lips in a deep good night kiss that left them both breathless. "The honeymoon can't start soon enough for me, sweetheart," he said as his lips trailed kisses down her neck.

Lolly broke free and stepped back. "Something to look forward to. And now to get my munchkin and me to bed!"

CHAPTER 13

"Okay, gang, we ready for tonight?" Sandy asked, addressing his two comanagers and the kitchen crew.

"As ready as we'll ever be back here," Meryl said. "Ms. LaSalle's chef is bringing the cake and a bunch of appetizers at three, and we've got the dinner under control."

"And the take-out orders?" he asked. Since they'd closed the restaurant for the evening, they had decided to offer a small selection of take-out entrees and salads to their regular patrons or anyone who called for a reservation.

"About three dozen, but we'll be okay. It's a limited menu, and we're prepped for it. We won't accept any new orders after two."

"Is it just Joe O'Leary we've hired as extra staff?" Sandy asked, looking at Murph. "I only ask because we've set up bars in all three rooms.

"We're covered, boss. If needed, either Rori or I can step in."

"I can jump in as well, but one of us should stay free." Sandy's dark eyes looked around at his staff. In its infancy, Field and Fire had already far exceeded expectations thanks to them. They had made it happen, each and every one of them. He cleared his throat. "I probably don't say this often enough, but I'm incredibly grateful to all of you guys for your hard work that's gotten us here. My best friend here," he said, placing a hand on Murph's shoulder, "we've been together for muchos anos, but even we couldn't have predicted back in the headiest Sandy's days that opening a restaurant would be anything like this. We didn't know what the hell we were doing, yet look at us now."

"It's all you, man," Murph said.

"We're a great team, all of us," his boss said. "So, I've decided to say thanks with holiday bonuses coming next week."

Sandy laughed as a cheer went up. "Don't get too excited. The bonuses won't buy you a yacht, but maybe they'll help over the holidays. Now let's get to work."

As the group dispersed, Murph followed his friend into the office. "You didn't tell me about the bonuses."

Sandy grinned. "Gotta have a few secrets from the nosiest person on earth."

"Do you need me to cut the checks?"

"All set. I had Andy do it last week," he said, referring to their accountant, Andy Roby.

"So you really are keeping it a secret."

"Yup."

"Okay, okay, I won't pry. About today. You should let Rori or me take over one of the bars if things get busy. You need to be a guest."

Sandy shrugged. "You know I like to keep busy. I mean, I like Loll and Jack, but don't know him that well. My invitation is swept up in the Morgan and Darn Yarner avalanche. On my own, I'd probably not be on the guest list."

"Me either," Murph said. "And Rori doesn't know them well either."

"Shush, don't speak too loud. She wasn't invited. Only you and me."

THE CHURCH WAS BEDECKED FOR THE SEASON, EVERGREEN BOUGHS TIED with red bows on the end of each carved oak pew and a massive silver basket of holly and greens on the altar. The Darn Yarners had decorated the building, including the wreaths on the outside doors and more greenery on the bannisters on either side of the stone steps. "Not half bad," Frankie Brown said to Helen Winthrop, Lucy's mother, as the friends and fellow Yarners entered the church. The sixty-somethings were a study in contrasts, Helen tall and slender, her long gray hair in a braid down her back, a plain gray wool coat with matching hat and a jaunty colored scarf round her neck, and her friend, with her curly gray hair and slouchy oversized hat and coat, resembling a Hobbit just arrived from Middle Earth.

Helen smiled. "We've had many years' practice." The Darn Yarners frequently decorated the chapel for weddings, funerals and holidays.

Jack's groomsmen stood at the entrance waiting to escort them to their seats. Jay Hallowell offered his arm to Helen and Robbie Faulkner, Jack's older brother, took Frankie in hand. Pete Santoro, Jack's foreman and the third groomsman, nodded as he returned from ushering a group.

J.J., the best man, already stood with his dad at the front of the church, chatting with Joe and Anna Goodspeed as Beethoven's "Moonlight Sonata" played softly in the background, the pianist hidden in the side alcove.

"How are you feeling?" Anna asked Jack.

"Great," he said, "but I'll feel better when I see her. She could have changed her mind this morning."

Joe smiled, placing a hand on his friend's shoulder. "How likely is that?"

A few minutes later, everyone was seated, the music shifted, and strains of Beethoven's "Ode to Joy" filled the church as the ushers, then Maisie came down the aisle followed by the three bridesmaids. The men were in one-button tuxedos, red bowties at their necks. Lolly had encouraged her bridesmaids—her sisters, Marla and Dara, and Lyddie—to choose a floor-length green velvet skirt and long-sleeved crepe blouses in a style of their choosing, and each wore a red sash around her waist, as did Lucy, the matron of honor. Each wore a sprig of holly in her hair. Maisie was in red velvet and black patent leather Mary Janes, a huge red bow in her hair. She held a basket of red rose petals, which she sprinkled carefully as she proceeded. Just before the altar, she slipped in beside her dad.

"Good job, baby," Sandy whispered, kissing the top of her head.

As Lucy reached the front and took her place beside the bridesmaids, the music shifted and the "Bridal Chorus" began. Lolly emerged on the arm of her father, Duncan LaSalle, dapper in his tux, not a hair of his snowy white mane out of place. The Broadway producer looked a decade younger than his seventy-seven years as he leaned over and said, "Here we go again, doll."

Lolly stifled a fresh remark as they began their walk down the aisle. Her dress was simple but elegant, a lacy bodice with capped sleeves above a flouncy layered crepe skirt. It suited her perfectly. She didn't wear a veil, but instead had a delicate crown of white roses, her hair flowing long and luxuriant over her shoulders.

"Wow!" J.J. whispered.

His father smiled, his eyes never leaving his bride. "That's one way of putting it."

Lolly had tears in her eyes as her father placed her hand in Jack's.

"Hi," she said shyly.

"Hello yourself," he said, fingers massaging her trembling hand.

As they faced the officiants, Anna leaned forward and whispered, "You look gorgeous."

"I'll second that," Joe said, smiling at her. "Shall we begin?"

Anna welcomed everyone, and Joe gave an opening prayer. The simple ceremony included readings from Dara, Lolly's sister, who had flown in from Paris for the weekend, and Jay. The couple had chosen to say traditional vows with a few added words at the end. They then exchanged rings, and Joe gave a short benediction, after which Marla joined her band, the Cherry Pickers, who were assembled in an alcove at the rear of the chapel. The band played the Beatles' "All You Need is Love" as Mr. and Ms. Faulkner took their first walk as a married couple.

When they emerged, it was snowing, and Lyddie brought a fur-trimmed white wool coat to drape over Lolly's shoulders.

"Thanks, sweetie," the bride said as she turned to Jack, his lips finding hers as bird seed mixed with snowflakes rained down on them.

"I love you," he said, as the crowd circling them clapped and cheered.

"Right back at you," she said, stroking his cheek. "I'm *really* happy right now. I hope you know that."

"I do, because I feel the same way, my love." He took her hand as they made their way to the Morgan's Fire farm wagon, all decked out with "Just Married," balloons, tin cans, and holiday greenery, wool blankets draped over the seat for the bride and groom. Gus Casey, farm manager, held the reins.

"If we don't freeze to death, we'll see you at the restaurant," Jack called to his family, then turned to help Lolly up.

CHAPTER 14

Most of the wedding guests were inside Field and Fire by the time Jack and Lolly arrived. A heater and blankets had staved off the chill, but both were glad to step into the warmth of the restaurant, fires blazing in each dining room, candlelight casting a soft glow on the dazzling rooms, each with its own tree and glorious decorations. The front room leading into the bar had been left open to accommodate dancing later, and the remaining space had tables with centerpieces of holly and greens, crystal glasses, silver flatware, and the restaurant's brand-new Spode Christmas plates.

"Incredible," he said, helping her with her coat and handing it to Rori, who stood to the left of the door. "I'm gonna check on my folks. They look a little dazed. Want to come with me?"

She followed his gaze to where the Faulkners stood by the bar, talking to their grandchildren. She reminded Lolly of Ruth Bader Ginsberg, short, petite, with white hair and sky-blue eyes. James Faulkner, like his son and grandson, was broad shouldered with a thick head of salt-and-pepper hair and emerald-green eyes. They were both active and loved to travel.

"You go," Lolly said. "I'm fine, and I want to find Maisie."

With a brief kiss, Jack headed across the room.

As if on cue, a voice behind her called, "Mommy!"

"Hi, sweetie," she said, hugging her daughter. As she straightened, she found Sandy right behind Maisie.

"Congratulations," he said, giving her one of his two-hundred-watt smiles as Maisie ran off to join a group of children at the far end of the room.

Talk about gorgeous in a suit that probably cost more than I make in a month, she thought, smiling. "Thanks."

"It was a beautiful ceremony."

"Thanks. Joe and Anna did a great job."

"As did you and Jack."

Lolly blushed. *Are we finally able to be friends and have this conversation?* she mused. *Happiness makes all the difference.* "Easy when you love one another."

"I'm happy for you Lolly. You look amazing, by the way."

"Thanks, that means a lot."

"There she is!" Richard said as he and Lucy came to greet her.

"I'll keep an eye on Maisie, no worries," Sandy said, nodding to his father-in-law as he stepped away.

As Lucy hugged her, then Richard, he said, "You're the most beautiful bride I've ever seen." He put an arm around Lucy and drew her close. "Except for my darling girl beside me."

"Thanks. Isn't this place is breathtaking tonight? They outdid themselves on the decorations, not to mention the tableware. Oh my goodness."

Lucy chuckled. "Tableware is what you get when a millionaire decorates for the holidays and the décor is all Pam, Rori, and Meryl with help from Greta and some of the kitchen staff." She didn't mention that she, Gail, Weezie, and Callie had also spent an afternoon decorating.

"Many hands," Lolly said, beaming from one to the other. "Thank you all."

AFTER A COCKTAIL HOUR WHERE CALLIE'S PLATTERS OF HOT AND COLD appetizers were served, guests found their places for dinner. Lolly and Jack had asked for the dinner to be buffet style, so tables were set up in each dining room, the doors between rooms opened wide, creating what felt like one enormous light-filled space. Meryl supervised as food platters, dishes, and bowls were arranged on each buffet. The entrees included many of Jack's and Lolly's favorites— beef Wellington, grilled salmon with cilantro basil relish, lobster tails, crab cakes, and Tuscan chicken with rosemary and herbs. There were also bowls of salads—Caesar, field greens and arugula and fennel with parmesan and a light lemon dressing. Baskets of breads from the local Moon and Stars Bakery were on every table, along with Field and Fire's fresh-churned, herb infused butters.

The serving tables laid out to her satisfaction, Meryl stepped back to observe the gathering. "Quite something, isn't it?" said a voice from behind her.

"Hello," she said, recognizing the now-familiar voice and turning to smile at Joe. *He has no idea how incredibly handsome he is*, she mused. "You look very dapper tonight."

"And you look very professional, and pretty."

"Just my usual white coat and chef's hat. Not too exciting."

He grinned. "On you, they are."

"Well, thank you." She could feel the heat of his nearness as her body temperature rose.

"Can I get you something?"

"I'd kill for a glass of wine, but I'd better not. A seltzer with lime?"

"Coming up."

Joe's fingers brushed her hand as he handed her the tall glass. As she accepted it, Meryl thought her knees might buckle under her. "Thanks."

"So this is quite an undertaking."

She nodded. "Field and Fire's first wedding reception. I don't want to speak too soon, but it seems to be going well."

"So far, it's going great. Murph tells me you're doing take-out orders tonight as well."

"Sandy didn't want to let down our regulars. We've got people who've been coming every Saturday night since we opened. They have standing reservations."

"Wow. I guess Murph's right. Whatever Sandy Rodriguez touches turns to gold."

She gave him a look. "Yes, even though I do like to think that some of us help from time to time."

Joe turned bright red. "Of course, I didn't mean to imply that—"

She laughed. "Just kidding. The boss is amazing. And he did grow up in the restaurant business with parents like Rosa and Cesar."

"I really am sorry," he sputtered.

Meryl smiled, lifting her glass in a toast. "No worries. Thanks for the drink. I really should get back to the kitchen." As she turned away, she felt somehow foolish for teasing him. *Were we flirting, or was it my overactive imagination?* she wondered, nodding to Murph as she crossed the restaurant.

"What's up with her?" Murph asked as he leaned against the bar.

Joe gave him a sheepish grin. "I think I might have just put my foot in my mouth."

Murph grinned. "I'm sure she'll get over it. Besides, I think our master chef likes you."

Before Joe could reply, a clinking of glasses signified the start of the wedding toasts.

AFTER MANY TOASTS AND LUSCIOUS DESSERTS, INCLUDING CAKE POPS, cupcakes, macaroons, and a stunning tower of choux puff pastry and crème-filled patisserie, a French dessert that was one of Lolly's favorites, the music began in the front room. Jack led Lolly into the open space as the band began playing John Legend's "All of Me."

"You didn't," she said, gazing up at him.

"I did."

"But you weren't crazy about this."

"Doesn't matter, you are. That's all that matters to me, baby. Come here," he said, taking her into his arms.

Tears streaming down her cheeks, Lolly leaned against his strong chest. "Oh, Jack, I never in my life thought this was possible."

"Well, you do have every John Legend CD ever made."

"That's not what I meant, and you know it."

"Of course I do, bride of mine. I thank the universe every day that I decided to rent your mom's cottage and we found each other. Truthfully, I'd rather be in our honeymoon suite instead this fishbowl, but with you pressed against me, I'm a happy man."

She felt him grow hard against her belly and smiled. "Thank goodness that fancy tux has a broad cut."

"I can control myself, no worries, but a guy can think ahead, can't he?"

"I'm right with you, husband of mine," she said, kissing him.

CHAPTER 15

"Home," Lolly sighed as the limo drove up the driveway past the inn to their cottage on Barnum's Ledge. "It feels like we've been gone forever, not nine days. I've never taken nine days off from work since Lucy and I started Merlin's Closet. I feel so guilty leaving her with all the Christmas craziness."

"She's had extra help. Besides, you had a good excuse for taking a break."

She leaned against him. "Hmm, you're right about that. Thank you for such a lovely honeymoon. I will miss our dear little love nest on that beautiful lagoon."

Jack took her hand and kissed it. "We have own little love nest right here. And we can go back to our island bungalow whenever you say the word."

"After we've saved our pennies, could we? Maybe not as romantic, but I'd love to take Maisie. She'd love it."

"And there are many Cook Islands still to explore."

As the limo driver went to open the trunk, they strolled up the walkway hand in hand, meeting Lyddie and her brother on the porch waving. "Cutting it a bit close, aren't you? We thought we'd have to start the open house without you," J.J. said.

"Are you dead after flying so long?" Lyddie asked, hugging each in turn.

Lolly laughed. "Are you kidding? In my first-class suite with its down comforter and comfy reclining chair/bed, I slept like a baby."

"Only night we were apart," Jack said.

"But we could visit since the units were side by side," she said.

"We'll help the driver with the bags. You two head on inside," J.J. said.

Lyddie added, "And Sandy just called. He and Pam will be by with Maisie around five. Says if you'd like a night to rest, they're happy to keep her, or your mom will."

"Absolutely not," Jack said, turning to his wife. "Unless you'd rather?"

"This is the longest we've ever been apart," Lolly said. "I want her here, home with us."

"Me too. First time our new family will all be together, especially since these two will be flying the coop tomorrow." His son and daughter were heading to Maine first thing in the morning to be with their mom for Christmas Day.

As J.J. and Lyddie headed to the limo, Jack said, "Well, Ms. Faulkner, shall we?" and swooped her up in his arms, elbowing the door aside and carrying her over the threshold.

"Oh, look what they've done," she said, gazing around at their beautiful living room awash with holiday bells, baubles, and greenery. Tables covered in festive cloths held silver bowls of holly, evergreens and berries. A full bar was set up in the tower nook that faced the water. A crystal punch bowl sat on a small round table, cut-glass cups surrounding it. A fire blazed in the hearth, and the dining room beyond was similarly bedecked. The wide circular dining table waited to be covered with platters, baskets, and bowls of finger foods. Jack's kids, along with Kendall, Mavis's chef, had been working for days on the food. They'd ordered breads and finger-sized eclairs, along with cookies and tarts from the bakery, but the rest was all their doing.

As Jack kissed her, J.J. came up from behind. "Hey, hey, not in front of the kids. So, what'd you think? Are you ready to wish everyone a Merry Christmas?"

"Son, I don't know what to say. You and your sister have given us such an incredible gift here."

"Jack's so right," Lolly said. "Everything is perfect."

"It's been our pleasure. In between the wild parties we've been throwing, we managed to pull it together."

THE PARTY IN FULL SWING, THE NEWLYWEDS HAPPILY SHOWED GUESTS around the house, and some of Jack's crew volunteered to lead tours to the inn across the snow-covered grounds lit up for the holidays.

"Incredible property," Richard Morgan said as he and Lucy chatted with Lolly and Jack. "If I didn't love Morgan's Fire so much, I'd be jealous."

"How was the trip?" Lucy asked. "I hear the Cook Islands are amazing."

"Heaven. There's no other way to describe them," her friend and business partner said. "So beautiful and untouched. Our bungalow was perfect."

"It was pretty cool," Jack said, arm around his wife as a new group of guests came through the door, among them Sandy, Pam, and Maisie.

"Mommy!" the child called, dodging guests as she raced across the room and jumped into her mother's arms.

"Oh, pumpkin, I've missed you so much!"

"Me too, Mommy." Maisie buried her face in Lolly's shoulder, finally peeking out to say, "Hi, Jack." a minute later.

He leaned over to kiss the top of her head. "Hi, sweetie."

"Daddy says I can stay here tonight. Is that true?"

"It sure is," Lolly said, setting her down and helping her out of her coat. "Kendall, Grandma, and Daddy brought all our things from the cottage, and your room is all set up."

"Can I see, can I see?"

"Of course," Lolly said, turning to her companions. "Would you all excuse us for a minute?"

Before she and Jack left for their honeymoon, Lolly had given her mother, Kendall, and Sandy detailed maps and instructions on the setup of Maisie's room, and Jack's crew had helped with the actual moving of furniture and belongings. They stored many things in one of the barns at Barnum's Ledge, then Mavis, Kendall, and Sandy set to work on Maisie's room. Murph and Joe had also come one day to help. Lolly's first glimpse of the room had been several hours earlier, and she was thrilled.

"Here we are, sweetie!" Lolly said, swinging open the door to the light-filled space.

"I love it, Mommy!" Maisie said, flopping on the window seat, gazing out at the dark water, an almost full moon shining. She had seen the room previously, but it had been empty. Now, filled with all her things, it came alive, magical and exquisitely designed.

After consulting her daughter, they'd decided to keep the beautiful antique white canopy bed and dresser she'd had at the cottage. The other furnishings were new and included a built-in desk that doubled as a vanity, beside it an arched window that overlooked the sea. All Maisie's toys and books lined newly built shelves, and her framed artwork adorned the walls and upstairs hallway. The south wall windows held dramatic views in all directions, and the tiny tower space had a window seat, under which were more books, board games, and toys.

"I'm glad you like it, baby," Lolly said, hugging her. "Shall we go down and say hi to the kids? I think I saw Sasha, Cameron, and Laura coming in right behind you and Daddy." She referred to the children of Ava and Dan Fielding, Richard's daughter, and her husband. Cameron was in Maisie's class at Cove Elementary. Dan and Jack had become friends over the last few months, bonding over their love of chess. They often met at the community center on chess night, then went out for a drink after.

As Lolly and Maisie rejoined the party, Joe came in with Murph,

Greta, and Rori. "Hello, welcome," she said. "So glad Sandy closed for the holidays so you could be here."

They greeted each other with hugs as Maisie ran off to join the other children. Jack took their coats, Murph assisting. They dumped their loads on the master bedroom bed.

"I'm surprised Meryl didn't come with you," Jack said as they headed back to the others.

"She's away for Christmas. Meeting her brother Johnny for two nights in Chicago. They're staying at some fancy hotel having spa treatments and have reservations at two of the city's five-star restaurants."

"Sounds like a chef's holiday to me. Her brother's a chef too, isn't he?"

"Retired. He's quite a bit older. He cooks for the Morgans' kids camp in Arizona in the summer months, but that's it. I think he made a bundle when he was working."

"That's right. That sounds like quite a place."

"Yup. Take Richard Morgan and plunk him in the desert and you're pretty close to it, I'd guess."

Jack chuckled. "Okay, the bar's down there and as you can see, there's food everywhere. Please help yourself. My boss just walked in so I'm gonna go say hello."

"Thanks, man," Murph said, going to ask Greta and Rori what they wanted to drink. He found them standing by the fireplace talking to Jack's parents, James and Ester, who were discussing her former restaurant, Winkler's, which she had co-owned with her ex-husband. Apparently, the Faulkners had eaten there on a trip to Westerly, Rhode Island several years earlier.

"My ex still owns it," Rori said, "and he has a great chef, so I'm sure it's still excellent. I'm happy where I am now. Much less pressure, much more fun."

Ester Faulkner nodded. "Letting go of the reins feels good."

"And bittersweet," her husband said, his green eyes warm, but with a hint of sadness.

"Jack's brother took over the gallery, right?" Murph asked.

Ester put her hand on her husband's arm. "Yes, and he and Davos are doing a great job."

"What do you think of the house and Barnum's Ledge?" Joe asked, deciding a change of topic was in order.

"It's amazing," Ester replied. "Jack is very talented, and he has remarkable vision. He can take a property and transform it into something no one could have imagined."

"How could he go wrong with a palette like this to work with?" James asked.

"Oh, I don't know," Murph said. "Most people would have torn down the inn and put up some monstrosity. Jack saw beyond that and preserved a local landmark while making it way cooler than it was."

"How long are you staying?" Joe asked.

"We fly to London the day after Christmas," James said. "It's been a holiday tradition since the boys grew up and flew the coop."

"Lucky you," Greta said, smiling at the couple. As she spoke, she held Murph's hand. *And lucky me*, she thought.

"So what can Joe and I get you all to drink?" Murph asked, gazing around at his companions.

Villagers of all ages came through, grabbed a drink and a bite to eat, and took the tour before slowly trickling out. The group had mostly thinned to Faulkners and Morgans when Joe said good night and thanked his hosts. "Great party, thanks, folks," he said, turning to walk out with Roland Jenkins, Jack's boss from Compass Properties. A silver fox with thick gray hair and piercing gray eyes, Jenkins was slender, medium height, dressed impeccably in a dark gray suit, over which he pulled on a charcoal wool overcoat.

As the two men headed down the walk to their cars, Joe said, "You must be thrilled at what Jack and his crew have created here."

"Mixed feelings. Thrilled, of course, but also conflicted as this project will most likely result in a Compass Properties loss. Not financial as we still own a percentage, but a developer and friend who I will really miss."

"Oh, I didn't realize."

Jenkins gave him a rueful smile. "No one does yet, but Jack's slowly buying us out of Barnum's Ledge and in the process, stepping away from the company. It was inevitable, but I'll miss him. Fortunately, I'm near to retirement, so my son and several other talented people will be stepping in, but it won't be the same without Jack."

"He is a wonderful person."

Jenkins nodded. "My wife of over forty years passed away three months ago, and my life has been work, so I don't have a huge circle of friends. Jack's one of them, and we had dinner several times a week when he was home in Boston."

"It's still very early in your grief," Joe said, his kind eyes studying the other. "Takes time to create a new life."

"As you're doing now?" Roland said, having heard Joe's story from Jack.

Joe smiled. "Yes, that's true. I don't expect I'll have figured that out for years to come."

"If you don't mind my asking, did you dislike being a priest?"

"Not at all. I loved it, but the past few years, something shifted, and I found I yearned for something else. To make a difference in another way."

"A courageous choice."

"Maybe. This is a very supportive community, so it seems like a good place to start my journey. Have you any plans for your retirement? Might they include more frequent visits to Horseshoe Crab Cove? You would always have a place to stay."

His companion chuckled as they reached the side of his Escalade. "Have you seen the owner's suite?"

"I have."

"It's mine exclusively to stay in or let out as I see fit."

"So there you go—an excuse to come back often," Joe said, extending his hand.

"You're right about that, thanks. And good luck to you, Father."

"It's just Joe."

"Joe, then. Good night and good luck to you. Have a good holiday."

"And you as well."

As Jenkins drove away, Joe stood gazing out at the water for several minutes before heading to his truck. *Figuring things out. Life's work for all of us*, he mused.

"You guys did good," Jack said, relaxing on one of the new sofas, surrounded by Morgans. The Fielding family had departed as had Sandy and Pam, but Richard, Lucy, Weezie and Wolfie remained, the latter sitting very cozily on another sofa with Lyddie, J.J. beside them. Gail and Tim had stopped by with his parents, then gone to Land's End, the Millers' farm, for supper. Rich, the oldest Morgan and his fiancée, Karen Miller, had done the same thing and were now dining with the Miller family. The elder Faulkners had gone to bed, and Lolly was tucking Maisie in.

"Thanks, Dad," Lyddie said. "Bummer that we have to leave so early tomorrow, but we'll clean everything up tonight."

"With our help," Lucy said.

"Oh no you don't," Jack said. "You have your family Christmas tomorrow. We're just hanging out, Loll, Maisie, and my parents. We're all going to Mavis's for dinner, so no prep or stress for us."

"In truth, Callie does most if not all of it," Lucy said.

Richard nodded. "And, as much of a party animal as I am, as usual, I have a lot of Christmas wrapping to do."

"Since he just finished his shopping before we headed over here," Weezie said.

"I know Lolly has some wrapping to do and toys to set up for Maisie. I'll help with the cleanup. Do you guys want any of this food?"

"Not with what Callie's prepared," Lucy said. "Which is always four times what we'll ever eat."

"What do you say, girlfriend?" Richard said, leaning forward to kiss Lucy's temple. "You ready?"

Lolly came down as they were getting into their coats, and Lucy hugged her. "What a lovely party, partner. Thank you."

"I didn't even get to ask about Merlin's Closet. I'm sure there's so much to do."

"Which we will not discuss until after the new year," Lucy said, giving her a stern look. "We're closed, remember?"

Weezie and a reluctant Wolfie followed their parents out. Lyddie walked out with him, and the young couple embraced. "I'll be back two days before New Year's," she said.

"Night, babe," he said, kissing her forehead and helping her into the car. Lucy and Richard observed the couple and exchanged looks as they hopped into the car.

An hour later, food stored, linens in the laundry room and plates, cutlery, and glassware washed and put away, Jack declared the cleanup over. He headed into the living room to admire Lolly's arrangement of gifts and one open present for Maisie, a beautiful doll and bed for her, carefully placed to be the first thing her daughter would see when she came down the stairs.

"Okay, Mama, ready for bed?"

"Sure am. Let me say good night to J.J. and Lyddie, and I'll be right there."

As they lay in each other's arms in their new home for the first time as husband and wife, Lolly sighed. "I love you."

"I love you more," he said, pulling her close.

"Hmm... Are you sure you're up for this?" she whispered, his erection against her tummy.

"As you can see, I am, indeed, up. Are you?"

"Always," she said as they began the already familiar, but always unique dance.

As Lolly stroked his hard cock, his hands moved up and down her luscious body, caressing her glorious breasts, moving between her thighs, fingers finding her lush wet warmth, moving in and out to find her clit. "Merry Christmas, my love," he whispered, kissing her earlobe. "Are you ready?"

"What do you think?" She guided him inside as they lay side by side, their bodies in perfect synchrony as he thrust deeper and deeper.

Conscious of their houseful of people, they stifled moans and cries as best they could, hoping no one was downstairs looking for a midnight snack. "Oh, oh, oh," she whispered as they reached a sublime climax.

As they collapsed against each other, Jack's hand on her ass, holding on to their sweet connection, he kissed her forehead. "Now I know it's gonna be a Merry Christmas."

"And the honeymoon isn't over, right?"

"Never, my love. Sweet dreams."

"You too," Lolly said as she closed her eyes, resting against his strong chest. She drifted off, still incredulous that she had found such happiness after so many years of loneliness and anger.

CHAPTER 16

"Welcome, Father— I mean Joe," Fiona O'Neill said as their former parish priest stepped in the front door. She hugged him tightly. "So glad you could be with us."

"Me too."

"Murph and Greta are here, and Darby. Alas, we couldn't persuade Seamus to leave his island paradise." Murph's younger sister Darby lived in Ohio and was home for the weekend. Younger brother Seamus live in Hawaii. Neither came home often, but she more than her brother.

"Hello," Murphy Senior called from the kitchen as Joe passed by into the living room. All three rose to embrace him.

"Good to see you," Murph said. "You remember Darby?"

She had her older brother's coloring, the freckles, reddish-brown hair, twinkling green eyes, and ruddy complexion. She also had his build. Sturdy was how one might describe Darby O'Neill, well suited for her job as an ER nurse. "Hi, Joe. It's been a while," she said, hugging him.

"Wonderful to see you, Darby."

His host emerged from the kitchen with a tray holding tall glass mugs. "This is O'Neill's original eggnog, but now alcohol-free. If anyone wants a drop, help yourself," he said, gesturing to a small bar holding various bottles of whiskey and rum. "We always used the Blackwell's rum, but suit yourself."

All accepted a mug, but no one rose to add liquor. It was the same scene that played out every time cocktails were served since Murphy Senior had given up drinking and sold O'Neill's Pub.

"This is delicious," Greta said. "The best I've ever had."

"Thanks. You're a bonnie lass," their host said. "Our Murph's a lucky man."

Over the family's favorite meal, roast lamb, new potatoes, and one of Fiona's signature salads, they discussed the latest village happenings and life in Bayport. "How are you settling in at my brother's duplex?" Darby asked, turning to Joe. The subject of his leaving the priesthood had not been broached.

"Very well. It's a great place."

Darby turned to her brother. "And when am I going to see Greta's place and meet Daisy the goat?"

"Anytime. Come later today, if you like. You're here for a couple of days, right?"

"Till next weekend."

"Oh, come for dinner some night," Greta said. "We'd love to have all of you, if Murph can get a few hours off?"

"Lunch might be better, babe," her fiancé said, smiling at her.

"I'd love to!" Darby said, forking several nasturtium leaves. The O'Neills specialized in growing exotic herbs, roots, flowers, vegetables, and fruits, which they supplied to restaurants and specialty markets as far away as New York. They now had a standing order from Field and Fire as well. Fiona was also a popular mystery writer who had come to the marriage with a sizable inheritance, so the family lived well and spent time with the things they loved.

Dinner things cleared, Fiona waltzed in, dessert on a silver tray, one candle adorning the top of her Irish cream cheesecake. "I know it's not traditional, but my family would kill me if we didn't have this," she said, looking at Greta.

"Merry Christmas everyone," her husband said, raising his holiday mug of coffee, topped with a mountain of whipped cream.

Family, thought Joe. *What a precious gift.*

"I'M SO PLEASED TO HAVE YOU ALL," MAVIS LaSALLE SAID AS SHE STOOD with Ester and James Faulkner in the great room at Netherfield Manor. Her home's name was an homage to Jane Austin, Mavis's favorite writer.

"What a place," Ester said, gazing around at the ornate gilded furnishings.

"Mostly for show," their hostess replied. "As an event venue, we have to keep up appearances, you know."

Jack chuckled beside them. "This is not your run-of-the-mill party house."

"I should say not," his father said. "I read a good bit about Horseshoe Crab Cove before we came this week, and this is one of the most exclusive wedding and event venues on the East Coast."

Mavis made a coy face, obviously pleased by her guest's remarks. "Not sure about that, but we do get our share of beautiful people, who desire and expect confidentiality. I think that's why we're booked for years in advance, because people recognize how private and secluded we are here."

"What do you do if you have a huge event?" Ester asked. "I know you have rooms here and the cottages, but people must have to book elsewhere for big events."

"There are some lovely B and B in the area, a respectable old inn in Southport, and now we're about to have Barnum's Ledge. That will be a huge help!"

"I see your daughter Marla, the musician," Ester said, "but is Darby still here?"

"Unfortunately not. She had to get back to Paris for Christmas week. She manages a very popular boutique. My son Duncan is in

New York with his father, but says he's coming to celebrate the new year. I'll believe that when I see it. Never mind, it's a blessing to have all of you and two of my children, and dear Jen too, who is like another daughter to me."

"You're fortunate indeed. And you have your adorable granddaughter."

"I do indeed. Speaking of Maisie, will you excuse me?" Mavis said. "I promised her we could do gifts now before dinner, as she's eating with her dad at Morgan's Fire."

For the next few minutes, wrapping paper flew everywhere as Maisie opened gifts from her grandmother, Kendall, Aunt Marla, and her mother's ward, Jen Honeywell. Clothes were bagged, and Maisie spent a few minutes playing with her beautiful new china doll, which her mother predicted would stay in one piece for a week or so. Kendall returned to the kitchen to complete the meal preparations, and Lolly passed appetizers as guests resumed their conversations. Fifteen minutes later, the front door opened, and Sandy appeared.

"Daddy! Look what Grandma gave me!"

"Merry Christmas, baby," he said, scooping her up in his arms.

Mavis turned to Marla. "Thank goodness. Our dinner was about to overcooked."

"Now, now, Mother," Marla said, eying her ex-brother-in-law. "Ooh, boy, he gets more gorgeous every day, doesn't he?"

"And doesn't he know it."

"Hey," Jack said, greeting the new arrival. "Have you got time for a drink before your next stop?"

Sandy grinned. "'Fraid not. Maisie and I are on a movable feast today. Our next stop is the Grille, then on to Morgan's Fire for dinner."

"That's right, your parents are open today."

"It's hard for them to take the day because Christmas dinner at the Grille has been a tradition for a lot of people around here. We have a huge family breakfast, and that's our celebration. My brothers and sisters help out, and there's a family table set up toward the back of the restaurant. They crash there in between working, and at the end of the night, they all have dessert and coffee together after the last guests depart. Struffoli and panettone."

"Sounds like a busy day."

"It is. That's one of the reasons I decided to close Field and Fire for three days. I don't want it to become anybody's Christmas tradition. Come on, baby," he said. "We gotta roll. Say bye to everyone and I'll get your coat."

Lolly approached the two men, giving her ex a brief hug before running her arm around Jack's waist. "Merry Christmas. You taking her now?"

"Yup, sorry."

"You and Pam still okay to have her tonight?"

"Absolutely. We're looking forward to it."

"Okay, then. I or we will come get her tomorrow."

"You relax. I'll bring her back after skating."

"That's right, the after-Christmas skate," she said, for a second sounding wistful. It was a Rodriguez tradition, a whole family skate on the pond behind Cesar and Rosa's house. "Sandy, I never adequately thanked you for your part in setting up her room. You all did an amazing job."

He grinned. "With your instructions and you-know-who directing, how could we not?"

Lolly rolled her eyes. "I hope Mother didn't drive you crazy. Thank you for putting up with that too."

"No problem."

"I'm ready, Daddy!" Maisie cried, now laden with a rolling pink suitcase adorned with unicorns, her new doll under one arm.

Sandy smiled as he helped her into her coat. "Here you go, pumpkin."

As the door closed behind father and child, Jack gazed down at his wife. "You okay?" A keen observer, he must have watched the interplay between Lolly and her handsome ex. Jack didn't miss much.

She smiled up at him and kissed his cheek. "Ghosts, that's all. I wouldn't want to be anywhere else but in your arms tonight and tomorrow and every day."

"That's good," he said, kissing her. "Because I don't intend to let you go."

A bell tinkled from the living room, and her mother's voice called, "Dinner is served!"

CHAPTER 17

The long farm table was set for twenty four. With its holiday greenery, festive linens, glittering silver candlesticks and flatware, sparkling crystal and holiday china, it was a Christmas card come to life.

"Oh my goodness, Callie. Everything looks lovely!" Lucy said as she admired the table that stretched from the dining room into the south end of the family room.

"A group effort," the cook and housekeeper said, smiling. "Helps to have many hands and beautiful things."

An enormous Frazer fir dominated the middle of the south wall of the family room. The two women stood together, gazing the length of the room and its various sitting areas, observing family activities. Ava and Dan's three kids along with Maisie were playing board games with Kyle and Weezie. Richard's four sons, Gerry, and Dan were clustered around the bar, Sandy and Richard chatted near the fireplace where a roaring fire blazed, and Gail, Pam, and Ava lounged in one of the seating areas on deep, comfortable sofas. Good friends, Karen Miller and Harriet sat nearby talking and laughing with Lucy's two children, Amy and Rob, who had recently arrived from their father's home. They always chose to spend Christmas Eve in the house where they'd grown up, then wanted to be with their mother and her large, boisterous new family on Christmas Day.

Lucy smiled. "This is Richard's dream come true, having his family all together on Christmas."

Callie nodded. "Yes."

"I don't know how we managed it, what with Gail, Tim, Rich, and Karen at the Miller's all day and Sandy and Maisie going here and there. I miss my mother, but this is a lot of people for her." Helen had gone to spend the holiday at her daughter Clara's, along with Lucy's youngest sister, Hazel.

"They're quite a group when all together, but lots of fun," Callie said. "I'd better get back to the kitchen."

AFTER A SUMPTUOUS DINNER FEATURING BEEF TENDERLOINS, LOBSTER tails, and grilled stuffed portabellas along with roasted vegetables and salads, Callie served her buche de noel and Christmas ice cream in the shape of wreaths, candy canes, trees, candles, and Santas. Meryl had created the ice cream shapes the previous week using antique molds passed down through her family. The oohs and ahhs as the beautiful desserts were served were the crowning joy of the wonderful meal. Weezie, Gail, and Pam helped with all the serving, and the Morgan boys were on cleanup duty. That way, Callie could enjoy the meal with her family she'd lived with for over half her life.

"Thank you one and all," Richard said as they lingered over dessert and coffee. The children were eager to run back to the tree, where a mountain of gifts still waited to be opened, but there was one more beloved ritual before the meal ended.

Long ago, Laura Morgan, Richard's first wife and the mother of their eight offspring, had proposed the idea of sharing holiday blessings at the end of Christmas dinner. They all loved the ritual so much that they sometimes shared blessings at other times throughout the year, but always at Christmas. There was no obligation to share, but space was given to anyone wanting to tell of something for which they felt blessed. Richard always began, then Laura and now Lucy as his wife, and then they went around the table.

"I'm going to sound like a broken record," Richard said, "but I can't say often enough how blessed I feel for my family, my beloved wife and her kids, as well as my eight, their significant others, and their growing families. Let's not forget my incredible grandkids!" He gazed over at Ava and Dan's three, winking. "I also feel blessed to have our extraordinary Callie, who takes such wonderful care of us and has been a member of this family for almost thirty years." Then he sat down, as he always did, with tears in his eyes.

Lucy stood and quietly gazed around the table, making eye contact with each person before saying, "I echo every word of my dear Richard. I feel so blessed that Amy, Rob, and I have been welcomed so warmly into this amazing family. I love you all very much."

As people spoke, mostly with simple thanks for the meal and the company, the sharing reached Harriet and Kyle. She said a quick thanks for the meal and then looked at her husband. He nodded, taking her hand and standing up. "As you all know, we're headed out to Saguaro for ten days to celebrate Christmas again and the new year. We have some news that we want to share with you all, as I'm pretty certain as soon as I tell my folks, they'll be on the phone with you. Harriet and I feel blessed and thrilled beyond words to be contributing to the village baby boom. We're pregnant." A cheer went up and more toasting, as Harriet burst into tears. Her sister rose and came around the table to hug her.

"Brave you," Lucy whispered, arms around her. "My love, you're going to be just fine. You're going to have the best care in the world, and you're going to be the most wonderful mommy in the world."

"Thanks," Harriet said. "I love you."

After the remaining diners shared blessings, Richard stood. "I love you all. Now we've gotta clear out all that stuff under that tree. Whattya say? Who's ready for presents?"

CHAPTER 18

Joe always loved the quiet and solitude of the week after Christmas. Multiple services and events behind him, he reveled in the peace and solitude of their aftermath. He had settled at Murph's, now comfortable and content. He was blessed with friendly, considerate neighbors in the LaFlammes. They'd had him over for a drink one evening before Christmas and were now away visiting family in Wisconsin.

Two days after Christmas, he sat reading the paper when someone knocked at the door. He rose to answer and found his landlord on the doorstep. "Good morning," Murph said. "I've got a load of firewood in the truck for you."

"Really?" Joe gazed out at the enormous load in the back of the truck.

"Yup. This'll last you till spring. I'm sorry it's a bit late. I usually get it all stacked by Thanksgiving."

Joe grabbed his boots sitting by the door. "Let me get my things on and I'll come help."

"I was hoping you'd say that. Half is for Gene and Lana, but it all goes to the same place. I'll be outside."

After several hours' work, the two men stood back to admire the huge, neatly stacked piles, Murph's truck bed now empty and swept. "Got time for coffee or something hot?" Joe asked.

Murph patted his shoulder. "Of course."

Mugs of hot chocolate in hand, the two sat near the woodstove, stocking feet propped up on the grate, a blazing fire visible through the stove's glass front. "Thank you for this," Joe said, gesturing around the room.

"You got it, buddy. I'm just glad someone's using it. I'm going to guess after we're married, Greta and I will live at her house. Maybe expand it a bit to include a bigger barn and workshop. It's such a cool location, not that the woods here aren't cool too."

Joe nodded. "Can't beat that view, and you've got your fenced yard for little Daisy."

"Who would have thought two people could love a goat like we do. She's so spoiled."

"Unusual breed. Tennessee fainting, right?"

"Yup. That's part of why she's spoiled. Everyone coos and fusses over her every time she flops over, me included."

"You and Greta seem very happy."

"We are. I feel so lucky. She's very patient with my moods and has been incredible as I've worked through the past and Aislan. Guess being a therapist helps."

"Being a kind, loving person helps more," Joe said, smiling at the young man he'd watched go through hell and back with the loss of his twin.

"Thanks, Joe. I don't know what our family would do without you."

"Probably just as you have always done. Supported one another and moved forward out of a terrible grief together."

Murph shrugged. "Not sure I'd moved anywhere before I met Greta and started to see Carroll, thanks to you." He referred to Carroll Ranglund, a therapist in nearby Bayport who he'd been seeing the past year. "You know, I can still feel her hand, her tiny little fingers holding mine. I didn't think I'd ever sleep again after Aislan died. We'd never been apart. Our beds were side by side, and we usually fell asleep holding hands."

"They say the twins bond lasts forever, even if siblings are separated by death."

"Carroll's helping me to understand that and learn how it can be a source of positive, joyful energy instead of aching sadness. But, enough about me. How are things going for you? Does your new life suit you?"

Joe smiled, stretching his lanky legs out in front of him. "Honestly? It hasn't sunk in yet. It was strange and somewhat lonely going through Christmas without all the services and gatherings. I did attend mass at the church in Southport several times."

"Not St. Mary's?"

"Not yet. Maybe sometime in the future, but I wanted to give Father Flynn space."

"So... I've noticed you and our fearless chef together a lot. Not that it's any of my business, but is there anything going on there?"

Joe drew his arms up behind his head, facing the blazing fire. "A budding friendship, that's all. Two fish out of water getting to know the village and community. There's a kindred quality in that."

Murph gazed over, arching his eyebrow. "Uh-huh. Is that what they're calling it these days?"

"Yes, and they will continue to call it that, thank you very much."

"She's interested in you, you know."

"As a friend."

"Maybe, maybe more."

"I'll leave it at that for now," Joe said, smiling as he thought of Meryl's lovely eyes.

Murph pulled on his boots and laced them up. "I'd gotta get going. We're open again tonight, and it's gonna be a crazy week. Stop by some night for a drink or dinner. Thanks for the hot chocolate and helping with the wood."

"My pleasure," Joe said, walking him to the door. He waved as Murph drove off wondering if there was, indeed, more to his relationship with the beautiful chef than he was willing to acknowledge.

Too soon, not ready, he thought as he shut the door against the cold.

MURPH AND SANDY CAUGHT UP OVER LUNCH. AS THEY PASSED THROUGH the main dining room about to head in separate directions, they spied Rori and Meryl at a table in the bar.

"Welcome back, ladies," Murph said, waving to his boss, who was heading off to town on errands.

"Thanks," Rori said. "Good to be back. I missed my little cottage, although I suspect Jack and Compass may kick me out before long." His comanager was renting one of the newly renovated cottages at Barnum's Ledge. Jack had agreed to let her live there until construction was completed, which it almost was.

"Oh yeah?" Murph said.

"I'm thinking of buying a condo in Southport," his auburn-haired comanager said. "But that's a little scary 'cause it means I'll be putting down roots."

"Is that the complex on the beach near Lindels?" Meryl asked, referring to the nursery that supplied most of the restaurant's plants and flowers.

"Yup, " her colleague replied.

"If I didn't love my little house on the river, I'd be tempted," the chef said.

"How was Chicago?" Murph asked.

She gave him a dreamy expression. "Decadent and sublime. Massages every day, great food, and lots of brother-sister time. We walked and walked all over the city. The lake is so beautiful in winter."

"Not as pretty as here, I'll bet?" he said.

"Different. So how *was* everyone's holiday around here?" Meryl asked.

"Low-key and fun. Greta and I went to my family. Joe joined us."

"Oh?" she asked, interest twinkling in her blue eyes.

"Yup, we've always been really close. He's spent Christmas with my family ever since he moved to Bayport right out of seminary."

"How's he adjusting to his radically new life?" Rori asked. "He's kind of a hottie for an older guy. I'm guessing women are buzzing around him."

"That's my cue," Murph said. "Gotta get the bar set up."

"Hottie?" Meryl said, raising her eyebrow at her colleague.

"Don't pretend you don't notice, girl. I've seen the way you look at him and he looks at you. I'm kind of jealous, if you want to know the truth. If you weren't so interested, I might pursue him myself."

Meryl rolled her eyes. "I seriously doubt he's ready be pursued or to pursue at this point."

"Don't be too sure. Someone's gonna snap him up. Mark my words."

Shaking her head, Meryl stood. "I've got to get to work."

"Don't wait too long, honey," Rori called over her shoulder. "He's not gonna be on the market long."

"Don't be ridiculous," Meryl said, pushing open the kitchen door. *She's right, of course,* she thought as she grabbed her white chef's jacket, *but what the hell am I gonna do about it?*

CHAPTER 19

A day before New Year' Eve, two white tents were erected and the Morgan's Fire event barn and tents were equipped with heaters, tables and chairs, and two large dance floors. Everywhere, thousands of twinkle lights were hung, and glittering gold and silver decorations brightened the rustic spaces. Richard's crews had been working for several days to set up what was to be a community New Year's Eve celebration.

Hands on hips, Karen Miller gazed around the party venue. "Look at this place! Your dad really should come out of retirement and become a full-time party planner." She and her fiancé were spreading tablecloths, then placing centerpieces on all the tables in the barn and tents.

Rich laughed. "Who says he's retired?" He pushed a lock of dark brown hair from his forehead, his green eyes warm as he gazed at her. Slender and tall, Rich had the dark bushy eyebrows of his father, but not Richard's gregarious personality. Dubbed "the quiet Morgan," he was an introvert like his mother, but also the bright, introspective, and creative CEO of Morgan Enterprises.

"Hey, you two," his father said as he came into the barn with another tray of table arrangements. "Won't be long before we'll be setting up for your wedding. Have you picked a date? You know, this space is always available should you decide to have the reception or rehearsal dinner here."

"Still thinking, Mr. Morgan," she said. After a lifetime of parental training, she couldn't break the habit of addressing him formally.

Richard grinned. "You know, when you do get married, you're gonna have to find another name for me. No member of this family calls me Mr. Morgan."

Karen blushed crimson. "I know."

Rich stepped between them. "I'll take those, Dad. Think it's too early to get all the plates and flatware out?"

"Nope. Full steam ahead. We're putting everything on the serving tables rather than setting each place since folks will probably move around."

Karen gazed around, marveling at the beautiful entertainment space her soon-to-be father-in-law had created with rustic wood-paneled walls, his-and-her bathrooms, and built-in bar and serving tables. "Thank goodness it's potluck. Did you ask people to bring certain things?"

"No. It's always fun to see what we end up with. Might be all desserts. Wouldn't that be fun?"

Rich shook his head. "Callie's making a bunch of entrees and salads so it all balances out. Come on, let's take a break and have lunch. This stuff can wait."

The couple retreated to the kitchen, where Callie had laid out pitchers of iced tea, lemonade and water, trays of sandwiches, chips, plates, cups, and napkins on the long, marble topped island. On stools at the far end, Gail and Pam had just finished their meal and were chatting.

"Join us," Pam said. "These BLT-and-avocado baguettes are out of this world."

"Where's Callie?" Rich asked, grabbing two plates and handing one to Karen.

"In town shopping," Gail said, "although I suspect she just wanted to get away from Dad and all his new ideas and whirlwind of suggestions. You know how he gets in full party mode. I swear Lucy left for work shortly after sunrise to get away. Merlin's Closet is on vacation and closed this week."

Rich said a silent prayer of thanks that he still had his rental in town. He loved being at the farm, where he had his office in one of the other barns, but he also loved escaping to his quiet home at the end of the day. "Poor Callie. She should go on a long vacation after this."

"She is. Didn't she tell you?" Pam said. "It's only ten days, but she and Kendall are going on a cruise. Dad and Mavis are paying. They offered to send them anywhere, but Callie and Kendall asked for a cruise."

"Where?" Rich asked.

"Mediterranean. Greece, maybe?" Gail said. "I haven't seen the itinerary. I advised them to go far enough away that Dad and Mavis couldn't call them back for a trumped-up emergency."

Plates loaded, Rich and Karen sat across from the sisters. As she took her first bite of a chicken salad baguette, Karen sighed. "You guys are so lucky to have a cook, especially one as fantastic as Callie."

Gail nodded, waving her half-eaten sandwich. "We sure are. Now that I'm at Tim's, I do miss this. I mean, Tim's a decent cook and I'm learning, but we're not Callie."

Her sister nudged her. "You have other things on your mind."

"Ha-ha."

"Seriously, though," Karen said, sipping the Arnold Palmer, half tea and half lemonade, that Rich had made for her, "my mom would kill for a Callie."

"Your mom's a fantastic cook," Gail said. She had tasted Faith Miller's food many times, even before she'd become her mother-in-law.

"Yes, but between the farm and all, she gets really tired," Karen said, her lapis-blue eyes wistful.

"Maybe she could find someone local?" Rich said.

Karen shrugged. "Maybe, but she's stubborn."

"Now, who does that sound like?" Rich asked, smiling

affectionately as he used his napkin to wipe a dab of mayonnaise from her curly brown hair.

"Ha-ha," his fiancée said. "Okay, Mr. CEO. You're officially assigned the task of finding Land's End a cook. Then following up by convincing Mom to hire him or her."

~

"You're the best boss on the planet," Rori said as she and Sandy stood by the maître d's table watching diners step in and check their coats.

"Are you going to the farm tomorrow night?"

"What do you think? I'm hoping there'll be some single guys there, including our newest hunky bartender."

Sandy laughed. "I suspect Joe isn't quite ready to date."

"Baloney. Now, if you'll excuse me," she said, stepping forward to greet the group.

Sandy headed into the bar and found Murph conferring with the two bartenders, a smattering of guests at the bar and tables near the window. "All set?" he asked needlessly. His friend and comanager was always on top of things.

"Yup. May have to make a winery run later, but we're probably okay. I have Wolfie on call, but he also gave me the key this morning."

"Thanks, man. So are you and Greta going to the big New Year's bash?"

"Of course, don't want to miss it. We may just go for a little while. It's our first New Year's together, and we kind of want to celebrate midnight at home, just the two of us. That is if we can stay awake that long."

"I hear you, man. Pam and I feel the same way, that is if my father-in-law doesn't guilt me into staying. Much as I love the farm, there's nothing like toasting the new year on a deck by the water. Reminds me of the Sandy's New Year's Eves."

Murph smiled. "Those were the days, huh? Two single guys, a few drinks under our belts, gazing up at the stars."

"Speaking of singles, did you know Rori has her eyes on Joe?"

Murph rolled his eyes. "She's not the only one. Poor Joe."

"I thought maybe he and Meryl had something percolating?" his boss said.

"Maybe. I think he's still in the 'figuring out my life' stage."

"Well, he's a single, good-looking, nice guy, so I guess there'll be a lot of ladies interested in knowing him better." Sandy gazed over his shoulder. "Dining room's filling up. Better go see if I can assist."

Poor Joe is right, Murph thought, spying his fellow comanager escorting a group to their table.

CHAPTER 20

"Do we have to go out New Year's Eve?" Jack asked, pulling his wife onto his lap. He was sitting in his favorite chair, one of the few pieces he'd brought from his Boston condo. Most of the furniture, except for a handful of family pieces, his personal belongings, and his chair, had been left behind when he deeded the condo to his former girlfriend, Marsha. His kids had gone nuts, but Jack had needed a clean break. "Maisie's at Pam and Sandy's, right? You know what that means?"

Lolly rested her head on his shoulder. "Oh? Do tell."

"We can make love in every room. Isn't that what you're supposed to do with a new house, christen every room?"

"Mmm... I love the way you're thinking." She nuzzled closer, smiling as she felt him grow hard under her. Maisie had spent the day with Mavis, but was back home now, playing in her room. It was nearly six and Lolly had been at Merlin's Closet all day with her partner.

"Come on... Let's stay in, just you and me."

"We have to make an appearance. Maisie's going, and she's dying to see all her little friends. This event is huge."

"Okay, let's make a pact. When Maisie leaves with her dad or maybe my mom, you and I will come home."

"Sounds like a plan," he said, capturing her lips in a deep, luscious kiss with lots of tongue and wandering hands.

As he caressed her breasts, teasing her nipples to hard, ripe buds, she pushed back, afraid Maisie would suddenly walk in. "Down, Tiger. I've got to think about dinner."

"All set," he said, hands wandering lower, rubbing her between her legs till she was panting.

Breathless, she met his eyes. "What?"

"I can cook, you know, and as you and I had agreed to do, I actually took this week off so I had time on my hands."

"I know... I'm sorry. Lucy had to get away from the party frenzy. That's one thing she doesn't share with Richard, the zest for entertaining large crowds at the drop of a hat."

"Richard's something, isn't he?"

She nodded. "Yes, he's one of a kind. Lucy told me once that when his first wife died, Richard morphed into the role of event planner as a way to move past the grief."

"Running scared, I'd imagine," Jack said, trailing kisses down her neck, unbuttoning the top of her flannel work shirt.

"Something like that. Now what exotic, gourmet dinner have you created for us?"

"Linguini with clam sauce. I have meatballs and red sauce too, if Maisie would prefer?"

"Actually, she loves linguini and clams. My daughter has a very sophisticated palate after a lifetime spent around my mom and Kendall."

"I'll set the table."

"Good," she said, hopping up. "Because another minute of what you're doing and I'd have to drag you into the hall closet, lock the door, and tear your clothes off."

"Sounds great! Can we do that?"

"No lock on the door yet, sorry," she said, sashaying off toward the kitchen, her glorious ass swaying to and fro.

"Hmm... Installing that lock is my next house project! I'll see you later in our beautiful new bed, Ms. Faulkner," he called as she disappeared.

Jack leaned back and smiled. Cynthia, his first wife, had kept her maiden name, and he would have been fine with whatever Lolly decided, but he had been so pleased when she'd wanted to take his name. It felt great to say it aloud. *Ms. Faulkner. It connects us*, he mused. *I love that we're family in body, soul, and name.*

BOXES IN HAND, JOE CLIMBED THE STEPS OF THE RENOVATED VICTORIAN two-story across from Laura's Community Garden.

"Back here," a voice called. As he opened the front door, Andy Roby, the accountant who owned the building, popped his head out of a room at the back end of the building. "You must be our newest tenant. I'm Andy."

"Great to meet you. Joe O'Leary."

Andy gave him a firm handshake. "Welcome! Pam and Elise told me a little of your story. I expect you're on quite a journey."

"Something like that." Joe smiled at the short, pudgy accountant with sandy-blond hair and warm green eyes. Dressed in rumpled khakis and a blue work shirt, he looked to be in his early thirties.

"You're a braver man than me. I'm a lapsed Catholic and live in fear of damnation after years away from the church. Can't imagine what you're going through."

"It's a process," Joe said. "I've been contemplating a change for a number of years. I still go to mass and can't imagine not continuing to do so."

The other man met his eyes as if considering his next words carefully. "I'd really like to talk with you about this in more depth once you're settled in and I don't have a client coming in ten minutes. Did Pam and Elise show you the office space when you were here last week?"

Joe shook his head. "The door was locked."

"Follow me. It was only locked 'cause I used it for storing clients' files and stuff. I've cleaned out my closet and moved everything out so you're all set. Had a set of keys made for you. Did the gals tell you there are two other tenants upstairs? Acupuncturists. We all use the first-floor waiting room you just passed through as well as the kitchen off the waiting room. "Here we are," he said, swinging the wood-paneled door aside. "It's a happy circumstance that the building has great soundproofing and these solid doors. It's a small space, but has those huge windows and the best view in the building. We painted every room including this one when we moved in. If you don't like the color, go ahead and change it."

Roby was right. The room was small, but light and airy. The windows looked out on an overgrown and wild-looking garden covered with its winter blanket of snow. It reminded Joe of the gardens he'd seen in his travels to England and Ireland. A table and chair sat in one corner, but otherwise, the space was empty.

"Do you have furniture you'll be bringing?"

"Some."

"Well, those can go too," he said, pointing at the table and chair. "You're welcome to go up to the attic and see if there's anything there you'd want to haul down. I bought the building furnished, and whatever my tenants and I couldn't use went up to the attic."

"I just might take a peek, thanks." Joe set his boxes on the floor and gazed around. "This will do very nicely."

"I'll go grab your keys, then I've got to get ready for my very demanding client who hasn't heard that most people take off the week between Christmas and New Year's." He returned two minutes later and handed Joe the keys. "Attic's a walk-up, door at the top of the second-floor stairs. That round key opens that lock as well as your office. The other one's for the front door."

"Thanks, again."

"Happy to have you. Will be a change to have a guy in the building with all these women."

As Roby disappeared, Joe sat and envisioned the space and how he might furnish it. *Two comfortable chairs, a rug, and a couple of tables should do it,* he thought, *maybe a quick check of the attic before I make the trip to the secondhand furniture store in Bayport?*

As he climbed the attic stairs, he mused on the life he'd led and what the future might hold. Since his college years, his living spaces had been furnished for him, as was Murph's little duplex. This was a novel experience for him, along with almost everything else in the past few weeks.

He rummaged around in the dusty attic, crowded with furniture, boxes, and lamps. He selected several small side tables, a worn kilim rug, and two floor lamps, setting them by the stairs. Just as he readied to descend, he spied a Victorian love seat covered in a navy brocade. Blanketed with dust, it appeared to be in relatively good condition. While pieces like it tended not to be very comfortable, he thought if he had a couple come in, they might like to sit together. He pulled off the sheet covering it and sat down.

"Not bad," he said aloud. Much more comfortable than he'd anticipated. He stood and lifted it, making his way to the stairs. *Quite a good haul,* he thought. *Thank you, Andy.*

After bringing everything down from the attic, he rolled out the rug and sat looking out at the garden, planning the next phase of his move-in. He liked the sage-green walls and polished wooden floor. *One more upholstered chair and an electric teapot oughta do it.* Murph had given him the contact information for the cleaning service they used at the restaurant. He called and made arrangements to have them come with their rug and upholstery cleaning tools the following week. He planned to begin seeing clients in two weeks and had already booked several appointments.

He locked up as he departed, although there really wasn't much of value in his boxes. Andy's door was closed, so he headed out of the silent building, satisfied with his progress. *'Twill be a good space for my new avocation,* he thought as he pushed open the glass paneled front door into the wintry day.

CHAPTER 21

Gail and Tim stood at the kitchen door with Lucy and Richard, gazing out at the light-filled spaces, their twinkle lights sparkling in the twilight. "Looks beautiful, you guys," Tim said. "Wish my mom and dad could be here. They're real sorry to miss it."

"But they're having a ball, I'm sure," Lucy said, smiling at him. "They've really caught the travel bug, haven't they?"

"Sure have. My sister Karen was nagging them about getting a cook before they left yesterday, but Dad said it was either traveling or a cook, and they chose travel." After a life spent working their farm from dawn till dusk, Rex and Faith Miller had taken several trips in the past few years and were currently in Italy on a three-week tour.

Lucy smiled at her stepson-in-law. "My mom's sorry to miss it too, but traveling to Saguaro with Harriet and Kyle in Spark's private jet was too much to pass up." Billionaire Spark Foster, Richard's older brother's college roommate, business partner, and now neighbor in Saguaro Valley, had developed a warm, close friendship with Lucy and Harriet's mother, Helen. The two flew back and forth to see each other as often as possible.

"We'll get 'em next year," Richard said, his arm circling Lucy's waist. "For now, we've got quite a crowd comin' soon so brace yourselves. Where are your brothers and sisters anyway?" he asked, looking at Gail.

She shrugged. "Probably hiding somewhere until showtime."

"Hey, Dad," Weezie said, coming up behind them. "Looking for me?"

"Always, Punky."

"Please don't call me Punky tonight, okay? Is Coop coming?" she asked, turning to Tim. She referred to Tim's best friend and shop mate. The village blacksmith, Coop shared workshop space in town with Tim, where Tim built his furniture and Coop plied his trade.

"Don't know," Tim said, "but your brother-in-law and Pam just walked in," he said, pointing to the side yard where Sandy and Pam strolled hand in hand. "He was in the shop today ordering a couple of lamps. He might know."

"Humph," Weezie said. She and the farm's veterinarian, Kiki Bloom, were in competition for the attentions of the village smithy. Kiki was away visiting family for New Year's and wouldn't be coming tonight.

Lucy exchanged looks with her husband. "I'm going to help Callie. Oh, Richard, there's the band now. Do you and Weezie want to show them where to set up?"

They'd hired the Cherry Pickers, a local bluegrass band that included Marla LaSalle, Lolly's sister and her boyfriend Richie. Richard waved, and he and Weezie walked out to greet them.

"Oh boy, here we go," Gail said as she and Tim strolled out to the tent.

BY SEVEN FIFTEEN, TABLES UNDER THE TENT AND IN THE BARN GROANED with food. Covered casseroles, whole turkeys and hams, roasted vegetables in chafing dishes, salads, breads, and pasta. Two dessert tables held cakes, pies, and platters of Christmas cookies. Since seating filled up fast, people tended to grab plates upon arrival and find a table. With the tent flaps down, high-tech heaters kept all dining spaces warm. The Yarners quickly found a table together. Their number was down with Helen and Faith away, but Faith's sisters, Hope and Grace, joined Frankie and Mavis. Rosa, Sandy's mom, and her husband, Cesar, had promised to make a brief appearance, but tonight was a big one at the Grille.

Kids were everywhere, running from tent to barn, playing in the snow-covered yard, flying back and forth to the horse barns. Lolly and Jack watched Maisie from the warmth of the barn, wondering how they'd ever tear her away. As they stood arm in arm, her mother came up beside them. "I just told Sandy I'll take Maisie tonight. Then you young people can have fun. I plan to stay till about ten, so I may need you to round her up."

"Will do," Jack said. "This is some party, huh?"

"Not my style, but Richard does love his barns," Mavis said, waving as she strolled off toward the bar.

"She's just jealous that there's another person in town who can throw parties as lavish and huge as hers. Look, there's Joe."

Jack followed her gaze. "He looks a little lost, poor guy."

"I'm going to catch up with Marla before they start playing. I'll find you for a dance in a bit, okay?"

"You better." Jack headed to where Joe stood, plate of food in hand, surveying the scene.

"Hey, man, can't find a table? Come on." He led his friend into the kitchen, and they sat on stools.

"Thanks. I got tied up with a former parishioner who wanted to talk. You already eat?"

Jack nodded. "An hour ago. I understand they try to get everyone fed early while the food's hot. Also cuts down on too much drinking on empty stomachs."

"Good idea. Must be tough to monitor that with a crowd this size."

"Lolly told me they have a crowd-control team. They circulate constantly checking to see what state people are in."

"Oh?"

"The Morgan brothers, Teddy's partner Gerry, Tim and Sandy.

Between them, they tell me that no one gets past their limit or if they do, they don't drive themselves home."

As strains of a bluegrass melody reached them, Joe ate his last bite. "That was unbelievable. Don't often eat like that."

"There's plenty more."

Joe laughed. "I'm full, although I might grab a piece of pie later."

The two men strolled out to rejoin the party to find Pam and Elise Nolan talking near the tent door.

"Hello, ladies," Joe said.

"Hi, Joe, how are you?" Pam said. "Did you get into your new space?"

"Sure did, and I even managed to scrounge some furnishings from the attic."

Elise frowned. "Oh, poor you. Wasn't everything covered with cobwebs and six inches of dust?"

"Yup, but I hauled everything down, and I have a cleaning service coming next week. Only need one more chair, and I'll be all set."

"You should ask my dad. He has a huge room in one of the other barns with furniture stacked to the ceiling. He just accumulates stuff and doesn't know what to do with it. When he and Lucy merged households, even more stuff got piled on. There's surely a chair or two up there. The storeroom is next to my brother Rich's office. He can show you."

"I would hate to impose."

Pam gave him a look. "Have you met my father? He'd like nothing better than to pawn off some of his treasures on you."

Joe laughed. "Thanks."

"No worries. I'll mention it to him, and he'll be nagging you to come shopping before you know it."

"Hey, everyone," Rori said, greeting them.

"I'm not sure you know my partner, Elise Nolan," Pam said. "Elise, this is Rori, Murph's comanager at Field and Fire."

"Great to meet you," Rori said, shaking her hand. "You're both therapists, right? I could use your services."

"Joe's joining us too," Pam said, smiling.

"Well, that might be tricky," Rori said, giving Pam then Joe a coy look. "Care to dance?" She held out her hand to him.

Murph, Greta, and Meryl observed Rori dragging Joe onto the dance floor. "Hmm... Looks like Joe's popular tonight," Greta said. "And what's gotten into your comanager?"

"That's just Rori being Rori," Murph said. "She announced she was going to dance with every single guy in the place tonight, and it looks like Joe's her next victim."

Meryl's face turned white as she stood watching the man she found so intriguing attached to her coworker. Her heart sank. *So much for a romance that never happened*, she thought.

As the song ended, Richard stood on a chair in the center of the party, clinking a glass. "Great to have everyone here. We've just put cups of champagne on all the serving tables. We'd like to toast the new year now, at nine thirty, so everyone is still with us. Please grab a glass and join me for a Happy New Year toast!" He hopped down, grabbed Lucy and two cups, and waited several minutes.

When everyone seemed to have a cup, he called out, "Happy New Year!" First, he kissed Lucy, then raised his cup in toast to all.

Couples were hugged and kissed, kids cheered, and paper horns tooted. After their dance, Joe had excused himself and slipped away from Rori. He wanted to find Meryl to say hello before he headed home. When Richard called for people to grab their champagne, he took a cup and turned to find her taking a cup beside him.

"Oh, hello," he said, smiling. "I was hoping to see you before I left."

Her warm eyes met his. "So early?"

He gave her a sheepish grin. "Truth is, I'm not much of a party animal."

"Me either."

As Richard again invited everyone to toast the new year, Joe smiled at her, raising his glass. "Happy New Year, Meryl."

She tapped her cup to his. "Happy New Year, Joe."

They each took a sip, and before she knew what she was doing, Meryl stood on tiptoes and kissed him. What was even more surprising, he kissed her back. As they broke apart, she looked up to find him beet red. "Oh, I'm so sorry. I don't know what came over me."

Joe reached out and lightly touched her cheek. It was soft, just as he'd imagined it would be. "No apology necessary. I'm honored." The music began again, a lilting waltz that was familiar to him, but he couldn't remember its name. "Would you dance with me?"

They both set their cups down, and she gave him her hand. Her warmth coursed through him, its effect like nothing he'd experienced before. Out of the corner of his eye, Joe glimpsed Elizabeth and Nathanial, the elderly couple from the garden. She waved, then winked, before magically disappearing into the night. He turned away and drew Meryl close. *Whether this will be a friendship or something more, I'm home.*

Richard stood at the edge of one of the tents, his arm around Lucy's shoulders. "That's a beautiful sight, isn't it? All these couples dancing with their sweeties."

"What about you and your sweetie?" she asked, head resting on his shoulder. Lucy had to pinch herself sometimes to be sure her happiness was real. Four years ago, her life seemed to be over after a cheating husband had taken her home, her dignity, and her heart. The love of her life, Rob Brennan, abandoned her for a twenty-two-year-old. They now lived in his family home, the home on which he and Lucy had lavished so much care and attention over the years. *Now I'm standing beside the true love of my life.* In Richard, she had found her soul mate, a kind, generous man, an extraordinary lover, and a devoted family man.

Richard laughed, kissing her temple and drawing her closer. "This sweetie will be back on the dance floor after he catches his breath. I love you."

"I love you too."

"Hey, check out my Wolfie? He and Lyddie are getting very cozy."

She chuckled. "Young love. Ain't it grand?'"

"You're speaking from experience?"

"Yes, at forty-four, I feel like they look. Young and in love with the man of my dreams. How did I get so lucky?"

"Back atcha, my love. Just think, by this time next week, we'll be in the Maldives, lying on a pure white sandy beach."

"Mmm, that sounds like heaven."

"Did I tell mention that it's our own private beach so bathing suits are optional?"

"Mmm... Getting better every minute. Can't wait to see your overall tan, gorgeous."

"Old-man tan, but who cares? I'll be beside my sweetie, who truly *is* gorgeous."

"Aw, you're making me blush, Richard Morgan. Aww... Look at Meryl and Joe. So happy for both of them. I knew there was something happening there."

Richard gazed over at the couple wrapped around each other as they swayed to "Cove Nights," a lilting ballad and one of the band's original songs. "He moves fast, doesn't he? Doesn't look like he'll be single very long."

"I'm glad. He deserves happiness, and so does she."

As a new song began, Richard stepped back and made a mock bow, holding out his hand. "Milady, would you care to have this dance?"

"I thought you'd never ask, milord."

Lucy did a mock curtsy, then took his hand, allowing him to spin her around and out onto the dance floor.

CHAPTER 22

Lolly and Jack walked Maisie out to her grandmother's car. "Night, Sweet Pea," she said as Maisie strapped herself into the booster seat. "Be good for Nana."

"Night Mommy, night Jack."

As they stepped back from the car, Sandy jogged out to say good night. "See you tomorrow pumpkin."

"Night, Daddy."

Mavis rolled down the Mercedes's window. "She's fine with Kendall and me. We have lots of plans for tomorrow. You all have a relaxing New Year's Day."

As they walked back to the party, Jack turned to Sandy. "Doesn't sound like you'll be relaxing with the crowd coming to the restaurant.

The other man shrugged. "Business as usual. You guys ought to stop by."

"Aren't you completely booked?" Lolly said.

"Not for family. Call and let Rori or Murph know you're coming and we'll put up a table in the kitchen, if needed."

"Thanks, but we'll probably hang at home," she said.

As they circled the house, their path lit by strings of twinkle lights and state-of-the-art exterior lights, Sandy said, "That's right. Lyddie's still home."

Jack chuckled. "That's a laugh. Now that she's head over heels in love with your brother-in-law, we hardly see her. Plus, I think she's waitressing for you tomorrow, right?"

Sandy shrugged. "Probably. We sure need her. Murph and Rori would know."

"So what happens for the rest of the night now that the champagne toast is over?" Jack asked as they stepped into the warmth of the barn.

"Bar shuts down around ten except for soft drinks and coffee. I think they put out snacks for the diehards. There usually aren't many people here at midnight."

Jack nodded. "Yeah, we're heading out as soon as we say our thank-yous."

"Believe me, Pam and I would be right behind you if I wasn't on drunk patrol."

"Good luck with that," Jack said as he and Lolly went to say good night to Lucy and Richard.

～

"What do you say?" Joe asked as he and Meryl stood watching the dancing. "You ready, or would you like to keep dancing?"

She smiled, meeting his beautiful dark eyes. "I'd have been long gone if I hadn't been asked to dance by a tall, handsome man."

"How'd you get here?"

"I came with Frankie Brown, one of the Yarners. She's my neighbor. Do you know her?"

"Tall, yet surprisingly hobbit-like? Good friend of Lucy's mother? Member of that Darn Yarner group?"

Meryl laughed her deep throaty laugh that he found very sexy. "The very one. She's my neighbor. Her house is very hobbitlike. Unfortunately, she left just after the toasts. I told her I'd catch a ride with someone, but now I'm not sure who."

"You're looking at him. I'd be happy to give you a lift."

Meryl set down her glass and took his arm. "I accept. Let's go say our goodbyes."

A LIGHT SNOW FELL AS LOLLY AND JACK ARRIVED AT HOME. "I'M SO ready for bed," she said, taking his arm as they climbed the porch steps.

"You and me both," he said, patting her hand.

"I never thought I'd say this, but I may be too exhausted for anything but sleep."

"I'm right with you. I'll be happy just to slip into bed and hold you all night," he said, unlocking the front door.

As it turned out, their naked bodies aroused at first touch, they found just enough energy. As they lay spent, he kissed her deeply, then whispered, "Happy New Year, Lolly. This old man feels very lucky to be lying here with you. You know I adore you, don't you?"

She smiled into his neck. "For an old man, you're pretty hot. *You* know that, don't you?" As she spoke, Lolly moved her hips rhythmically, pleased to feel his cock grow hard inside her. "And for an old man, you sure have a lot of stamina."

"You bet your sweet, luscious ass," Jack growled, beginning a slow, sensuous rut, every part of her turning him on. This time, their lovemaking was more languid, lips and hands finding the other's erogenous spots as they moved to another explosive climax. Lolly screamed out as her orgasm overtook her, all thought obliterated.

Afterward, Jack held her, planting soft kisses up and down her neck. "Wow, that was primal, babe. Your cries took me right over the edge. I was into them."

"They're my new thing," she said, kissing his strong jaw. "Total, blinding release. Couldn't have happened with anyone else in the house, so I seized the moment."

"Well then, here's to having the house to ourselves," he said as they drifted off to sleep.

"Another New Year's behind us, my love," Richard said as he drew Lucy to him. As they embraced and she felt him grow hard against her belly.

Lucy snuggled closer moving from side to side, caressing his erection with her body. "I know it's one in the morning, but I feel fully awake. How about you?"

"For you, always, my beauty. Care for a roll in the hay?"

"I thought you'd never ask." She rolled over to straddle him in a position they'd been enjoying of late. Swiveling her hips, she smiled down at him. Richard's eyes were closed. "Hey, sexy. You going to sleep?" she whispered.

"Not a chance." He reached up to caress her full, perfect breasts. Then lips replaced hands as he took one breast, then the other in his mouth, his tongue teasing her nipples to exquisite hardness.

Lucy lifted her hips and guided him into her wet, warm center, arching her back with pleasure. They began a familiar dance that never felt quite the same as they took each other to soaring heights, every lovemaking a new unique, precious gift. "Oh, baby!" he whispered, his lips everywhere as she thrust and gyrated above him.

"You like?" she asked, her tone bold and teasing.

"Baby, there's not a word in the dictionary for what I'm feeling."

"Happy New Year to my hunky husband. What did our little village do without you?"

"I'm sure you were chugging along just fine without the Morgan clan."

"Speaking of chugging, let's take this train to the moon and back, shall we?"

"I'm right with ya, baby!"

～

All bundled up, Meryl and Joe headed for his truck. She brushed up against him as they walked. "It's amazing how Richard's heaters keep the entire space—yard, barn and lawn—so warm when it's so cold here," she said as they rounded the house.

"You cold? Come here." Joe slipped his arm around her shoulders.

"Thanks," she said, her smile hidden under her thick wool scarf.

They were quiet on the ride to River Road. As they drew close to her little house on the river, Meryl said, "It's this one, right next to Hobbitville."

Joe pulled the truck into the drive alongside Meryl's blue Mini Cooper. "With that arched door, it does evoke images of Middle Earth, doesn't it?"

"You should see the inside. Someday, you'll have to visit, and we'll drop in on Frankie."

"I'd like that." Joe hopped out and walked her to her door.

She looked up to meet his eyes as they stood on the doorstep. "Want to come in for coffee or tea?"

"Thanks, but I'd best get going and let you get your sleep. I understand that the restaurant's booked solid tomorrow."

"Well, there is that. Thanks for the ride and the dancing. Thanks to you, I had fun at an event I was kind of dreading."

Joe took her hands. "Me too. I just want to say... I mean, I like you Meryl... I really like you, and I'd like to get to know you better. It's just right now, this...this dating stuff is all new to me."

"I know. Please don't feel pressured. Let's just agree to be friends and see where that leads us. Does that sound okay?"

"More than okay."

He leaned down and kissed her soft lips. As his tongue touched hers, Joe experienced an exquisite and novel sensation.

Finally, he stepped back to find Meryl's eyes sparkling with warmth. "If that was a friendly kiss, I'm going to love this relationship," she said.

Joe laughed, reaching out to gently touch her cheek. "Me too. Here's to a happy new year ahead for you."

"For us," Meryl said, as she hugged him.

"For us," he said, tears in his eyes. *For us, forever and ever.*

Read on for sample pages of *Joe's Calling,* book eight in the Morgan's Fire series!

JOE'S CALLING

Chapter 1

Afternoon light streamed into the space Joe O'Leary, ex-priest, social worker, and therapist, now called his office. He heard muffled footsteps above him, but otherwise, the old Victorian was silent. Peaceful. His last client had departed five minutes earlier and left the door ajar. Gazing out at the tangled garden behind the house, Joe leaned back, enjoying a last cup of Earl Grey before heading home. As he sipped the hot tea, he breathed in the scent of bergamot, fragrant, familiar, comforting.

A door opened in the hallway, and seconds later, his landlord, Andy Roby, popped his head in. "Hey, Joe, how're you settling in?" the accountant asked, his green eyes warm, sandy hair ruffled as if he'd been trying to pull it out. Short and a little pudgy, Andy had recently asked Joe if he'd like to be his running buddy. Ten years his senior, Joe was tall and lean. While his running days were mostly behind him, he had agreed, but they had yet to begin their exercise regimen.

"Great, thanks, Andy. I have about twenty regular clients and a few more about to begin."

The other man whistled, leaning his shoulder against the

doorframe, scanning the room. "Wow, so quick? Have you been advertising?"

Joe smiled. "No, most of them are former parishioners. We have a different kind of relationship than before, but there's a sense of security, I suspect, in knowing your therapist. I've asked that they clear it with the new priest, Father Flynn. I did as well, as I don't want to step on his toes. Care for a cup of tea?"

"Thanks, but I've gotta run. Blind date. My sister's fixing me up. I'm pretty certain it will be a disaster, just like all the others."

"You never know," Joe said. Andy, forty years old, was divorced with two teenage children.

"That's the trouble. I know my sister. The women she thinks will be perfect for me never are. It's become my Friday night torture. Have a great weekend."

"You too."

"And let's set a start date for our morning jog. Maybe next Monday? You game?"

"I might be able to manage a lope."

"That should work since you're at least a foot taller, so you have a longer stride. You can lope and I'll scramble to keep up. Night."

"Night," Joe said, amused by the image Andy conjured up.

For many years, his Friday-night routine involved picking up some kind of seafood takeout. Tonight, he decided to order a lobster roll from Bluewater Seafood, a popular restaurant near his house. He made the call, then leaned back in his chair to enjoy the remnants of his tea.

Invariably, in quiet moments, his thoughts drifted to Meryl Stockdale, chef at Field and Fire, the village's newest restaurant. *Meryl and her luminous blue eyes.* Months earlier, their lives had intersected over the holidays. There had been a spark, but it was too soon for him. Thus, by tacit agreement, they had gone their separate ways. *Is it time now?* He set his empty mug aside. He had strong feelings for her, of that he was certain. Whenever their paths crossed, his heart raced and his body temperature went through the roof. His feelings went beyond the physical, however. With Meryl, he glimpsed a home, a loving, nurturing home. Nowhere else, with no one else, did he experience peace and steadiness and the promise of a loving future.

Friday night was hopping at Field and Fire, the farm-to-table restaurant located on the vast Morgan's Fire property just north of the village of Horseshoe Crab Cove. Meryl tucked errant strands of sandy hair under her chef's hat as she surveyed the staff going about their work. She'd trained them well. She barely had time to appreciate how smoothly the kitchen was running before she got bumped from behind.

"Oh, Meryl! I mean Chef Stockdale, I am so sorry!" Lyddie Faulkner, one of their best waitresses, swung a full tray of entrées to the side, managing to avoid dropping them. In crisp white shirt and tailored black slacks, her blonde hair in a tight ponytail, she looked lovely as always, her pale cheeks now crimson.

Meryl smiled at the nineteen-year-old. "Good save. And you know it's Meryl, even when you're trying to run me down."

"I am so, so sorry. Are you okay?"

"More than okay. Now scoot or the food'll be cold."

As Lyddie disappeared, Rori Lake, the restaurant's comanager and Meryl's head chef, stepped into the kitchen. "What happened to the kid? She looks like a scared rabbit."

"We had a collision."

Rori flipped her long auburn hair to the side as she stared at the dining room door. "Doesn't sound like her. She's usually so cool, calm, and collected."

"Trouble in paradise, maybe?" Freddy Santos, the sous chef, remarked, as he added a handful of herbs to a platter of sautéed calamari. Meryl seldom put breaded and fried seafood on the menu, and the calamari was no exception. Lightly sautéed in olive oil, garlic, and a local farm's freshly picked sweet peppers, the dish was already a favorite of local diners and reviewers.

Rori turned to Freddy. "I'm sure there's a story there, but I can't stay to hear it. Later. Have either of you seen Murph?"

Her companions shook their heads. As she disappeared, Meryl looked over at her sous chef. "You really shouldn't give her any ammunition, you know."

"I know, I know," Freddy said, sliding the platter of calamari aside, ready to be picked up. "It was just fresh in my mind since she and her hot boyfriend were squabbling in the back hall a few minutes ago."

"You don't miss much, do you, nosey?"

Meryl eyed her dark-haired chef, his smooth skin a deep copper against his tall, white hat. Freddy missed little with those coal-black eyes and razor-sharp hearing. It was unnerving. Wolfie Morgan, the hunky boyfriend to whom he referred, managed the Morgan's Fire winery. His father, Richard, owner of Morgan's Fire, was an investor in the restaurant.

"It's a gift. Hey, while we're gossiping, I haven't seen the ex-priest around lately. Are you keeping him under wraps?"

Now Meryl blushed. "No comment."

"Wonder if we'll be needing an extra bartender anytime soon." Joe sometimes tended bar when the restaurant had private functions.

"Not funny. Besides, Joe and I are just friends."

"Uh-huh. I certainly don't look at my friends the way you two goo-goo eye each other."

"Back to work!" she said, heading down to supervise at the other end of the room.

Get *Joe's Calling!*

ALSO BY M. LEE PRESCOTT

Contemporary Romance

Mystery

The Ricky Steele Mysteries

Prepped to Kill

Gadfly

Lost in Spindle City

Poof!

Lady Love: A Cautionary Tale

Also, featuring Ricky Steele:

Jigsaw

Roger and Bess Mysteries

A Friend of Silence

In the Name of Silence

The Silence of Memory

Silencing the Pen

Well-Loved Romances

Widow's Island

Hestor's Way

Morgan's Run Romances

Emma's Dream

Lang's Return

Jeb's Promise

Rose's Choice

Hope's Wonder

Ruthie's Love

Polly's Heart

Kyle's Journey

Gus' Home

A Valley Christmas

Aria's Song

Tom's Ride

Bella's Touch

Morgan's Fire Romances

Lucy's Hearth

Tim's Hands

Pam's Garden

Rich's Dilemma

Lolly's Wish

Greta's Goat

A Horseshoe Crab Cove Christmas

Joe's Calling

Young Adult Historical Romance

Song of the Spirit

ABOUT THE AUTHOR

M. Lee Prescott is the author of dozens of works of fiction for adults, young adults, and children, among them *Prepped to Kill*, *Gadfly*, *Lost in Spindle City*, and *Poof!* (Ricky Steele Mysteries), *A Friend of Silence*, *In the Name of Silence*, and *The Silence of Memory* (Roger and Bess Mysteries), *Jigsaw*, and *Song of the Spirit*, and her contemporary romance series, *Morgan's Run*. And now book seven of Morgan's Fire, *A Horseshoe Crab Cove Christmas*, where favorite series characters and new ones come together to celebrate the holidays. In addition to her fiction, her nonfiction books are published by Heinemann, and she has written numerous articles in the field of literacy education. Lee is a professor emeritus at a small New England liberal arts college, where she taught reading and writing pedagogy. Her research focuses on mindfulness and connections to literacy.

Lee has lived in southern California (love those Laguna nights!), Chapel Hill, North Carolina, and various spots in Massachusetts and Rhode Island. Currently, she resides in Massachusetts on a beautiful river, where she canoes, swims, and watches an incredible variety of wildlife pass by. She is the mother of two grown sons and spends lots of time with them, their beautiful wives, and her beloved grandchildren. When not writing, Lee's passions revolve around family, yoga (Kripalu is a second home), swimming, sharing mindfulness with children and adults, and walking.

Lee loves to hear from readers. Email her at *mleeprescott@gmail.com*, and visit her website to hear the latest and sign up for her newsletters!

AUTHOR WEBPAGE AND NEWSLETTER SIGN-UP
http://www.mleeprescott.com/

FOLLOW ME ON BOOKBUB!
https://www.bookbub.com/search/authors?search=M.+Lee+Prescott

Please leave a review for this book!

I'm thrilled to bring you *A Horseshoe Crab Cove Christmas!* This marks the seventh *Morgan's Fire* book as beloved series characters come together to celebrate the holidays. A contemporary romance series, *Morgan's Fire*, follows a host of strong, resilient women—and men— as they live, fall in love and prosper in their New England coastal village.

Thank you so much for reading *A Horseshoe Crab Cove Christmas!* and returning to this close knit community with me. I love the village and all the colorful, vibrant characters who inhabit it. If you like *A Horseshoe Crab Cove Christmas!* and are willing to write an Amazon review, I would be very grateful. If you would like to sign up for future book releases, giveaways, and occasional notices about my books, please visit my Author Website *http://www.mleeprescott.com/* and sign up for my newsletter, then follow me on BookBub *https://www.book-bub.com/search/authors?search=M.+Lee+Prescott*. I promise I will not share your address, nor will I flood you with emails. Do visit my site to read more about my books and hear what's next.

Finally, this book has been revised, proofed, and edited many, many times, but my intrepid assistants and I are human,, so if you spot a typo, please email me at *mleeprescott@gmail.com*, and I will fix it. If you'd like to know more about my other books, please scroll ahead to the next section.

Warm wishes,

M. Lee